A+

SUMMER RANGE

**Center Point
Large Print**

**This Large Print Book carries the
Seal of Approval of N.A.V.H.**

SUMMER RANGE

L. P. Holmes

CENTER POINT PUBLISHING
THORNDIKE, MAINE

This Center Point Large Print edition
is published in the year 2004 by arrangement with
Golden West Literary Agency.

The text of this Large Print edition is unabridged. In other
aspects, this book may vary from the original edition. Printed in
Thailand. Set in 16-point Times New Roman type.

ISBN 1-58547-488-6

Library of Congress Cataloging-in-Publication Data

Holmes, L. P. (Llewellyn Perry), 1895-
    Summer range / L. P. Holmes.--Center Point large print ed.
    p. cm.
    ISBN 1-58547-488-6 (lib. bdg. : alk. paper)
    1. Large type books. I. Title.

PS3515.O4448S86 2004
813'.52--dc22

2004006287

Contents

1. Ides of Spring

SOMETIME DURING THE NIGHT CAME THE CHANGE OF seasons. Awakening to an unaccustomed warmth, Cleve Fraser threw back a couple of blankets and lay listening to the drip of water from the eaves of the ranch house. The spring thaw was on.

Reared on one elbow, Fraser built a cigarette, and after lighting it used the match's thin flare for a glance at the heavy silver case watch hanging on a nail by the head of his bunk. Five o'clock. Daylight would begin to show in another hour.

Fraser had been impatiently waiting for this thing to happen—the breaking of winter's stubborn grip. It had been a winter that had come early and stayed late. In the higher reaches of the Sentinels the snow had piled deep, and for months there had never been less than a foot of it on the benchland level around Saber headquarters.

That there would be some winterkill of the weaker cattle, Fraser knew, while the hardier ones would have been far drifted. Spring roundup would be a heavier chore than usual, but right now Fraser was eager for the drive and grinding toil of it, for he was restless from the long weeks of comparative inactivity.

He smoked out his cigarette, then got up and dressed in the dark. He felt his way out into the kitchen, lighted a lamp, and got a fire going in the stove. He put on a pot of coffee to cook and a pan of water to heat. He got out his razor and was beginning to shave when the back door opened and Soddy Joens, who had come across from the bunkhouse, stepped in from the dripping dark.

Soddy was long, lank, and lugubrious. He backed up to the purring stove and spread his hands to the heat.

"World's leakin' water from every damn crack and corner," he observed grumpily. "First it was snow we had to wallow through, now it'll be muck. Sure will seem good to feel summer's sun on the back of my neck and to drop in at the drag of a gather and get a lungful of honest dust."

Fraser grinned. "You're a hard man to satisfy, Soddy. More than once I've heard you cussin' dust."

Soddy grunted. "Man's got to cuss somethin' or shrivel in his own acid." He laid a dour glance on Fraser. "Hell of a time of day for a man to shave. You must be figurin' on town."

Fraser nodded. "Want to be on hand to see the fun."

The coffeepot began to rumble and steam. Soddy poured a cup, cradled it in both hands, and sipped cautiously. A thought came to him and his head swung up. "That's right—this is the day. You figure to put in a bid on Bunch Grass, Cleve?"

Fraser worked the keen steel carefully about the angle of his chin. "Not me. Where would I get the money?"

"Mebbe you could borrow it from Stack Portland," Soddy said.

Fraser shook his head. "Grat Mallory is going to get Bunch Grass, Soddy. He's got the money of his combine behind him. Only way Mallory could be kept out of the deal would be if all the outfits around the rim of Bunch Grass would pool their cash and buck him together. But they won't do that. For years they've been pulling and hauling over that government range, each one jealous of the other fellow. Which Mallory damn well realizes."

"Mallory closes them out of Bunch Grass they'll have plenty reason to pull and haul," observed Soddy darkly. "Without that range to work on they'll all be way overgrazed. Think they'd realize that."

"You'd think they would," agreed Fraser, wiping his razor and putting it away. He filled a washbasin with hot water, stripped to the waist, and scrubbed luxuriously. He looked a bigger man out of his shirt than in it. He was long of limb and heavy of bone, with muscles that lay smooth but solidly packed across his back and shoulders. The deep weather tan of his face and neck was in strong contrast to the whiteness of his torso.

His features were rugged, and shaving always brought out more markedly the thin scar line which ran from the temple halfway down the right side of his face. It was not a disfiguring scar, but it did add a slight cast of harshness to his expression. His hair was thick and brown, with a suggestion of copper in it, and his eyes held a granite-gray shine in the lamplight.

Soddy Joens continued to brood over his coffee cup. "We ain't never used Bunch Grass like the others, Cleve, so that part of it won't make no difference to us. But I'm remembering that some of our high meadows, like the Garden, rate as mighty fine summer range. And grass hunger is like money hunger with some men. They just never can get enough of it. Suppose Mallory, once he gets dug in solid in Bunch Grass, starts lookin' as high and far as the Garden, then what?"

Fraser shrugged big shoulders into his shirt. "Why,"

he said tersely, "it's just possible he'd find misery in the trail. But pour me a cup of that coffee and quit dreaming up troubles that may never come."

"Troubles always come," retorted Soddy pessimistically. "Man was born to them."

Day was breaking thinly through the timber when Fraser, up on a tall, line-backed dun horse, worked out the switchbacks of a down-running trail. Soddy had been right about the world leaking water. It ran amber brown and eager in every gulch and draw, and the dun's hoofs, cutting through the thinning snow, churned and slopped in it.

The swiftness of the overnight change was startling. Snow that had been a white and solid mantle was shrinking steadily, taking on the look of a garment worn out and falling apart with age.

Fraser broke from the last of the timber and into the long, open slope. Here the snow was only a few ragged patches, scabbing the earth, and across the far-spread reaches of the lower flats there was no trace of it at all. A sky which had for weeks been monotonous with somber overcast now lay clear from horizon to horizon and in the east was beginning to flush up rosily. It would, thought Fraser, be no time at all before the first eager green of new grass would stain the warmer slopes.

Stony Creek was all arumble with wild waters, and a number of white-faced cattle, shaggy in their winter coats, were prowling its willow-fringed borders. Fraser swung the dun over that way and read his Saber brand on most of them, deciding they were in very fair condition, all things considered. Several of the animals carried Alec Cormack's Shield and Cross iron and on a few Pete Jackson's Triangle P J showed. Which went to prove how winter's roughness could drift cattle, for the nearest limit of Jackson's range was a good twenty miles distant.

The sun came up and laid a bright glitter all across this wide, drenched land. Birds set up a cheery tumult in the creek willows, and in the far distance the white alarm hairs on the rumps of a little band of antelope struck up a drifting shine. There was a bustling breeze in the air and it was clear vigor in a man's lungs. The world was on the move to better days, and winter's bitterness was as if it had never been.

Fraser followed the run of Stony Creek to where it made its looping bend to the west. The crest of the furious soil-yellowed waters lacked only a few feet of lipping the stringers of the log bridge which crossed here, and the dun snorted with relief as it stepped again to solid earth on the far side. Half an hour later Fraser rode up to Alec Cormack's Shield and Cross headquarters.

A big, handsome sorrel horse stood under saddle at the corral fence, fretting with eagerness to go, and there also was Nate Lyons, one of Cormack's riders, hooking a team to the ranch buckboard. He grinned and lifted a hand.

"How! Mite early for a bear to come down out of the hills, ain't it?"

"Maybe," admitted Fraser cheerfully. "But this bear got restless. The family heading for town, Nate?"

Nate nodded. "Yup! Alec's goin' in to bat his head against a rock."

"The Bunch Grass deal?"

"That's right. Alec aims to bid on it, but he ain't got no more chance than I'd have. Grat Mallory's got too many pesos behind him. Some of us tried to tell Alec that, but you know how he is, Cleve. Stubborn old blister when he gets his neck bowed. You aimin' to mix in?"

"Not me!" Fraser's denial was emphatic. "I know my limits. Saw a few head of Pete Jackson's stuff over past Stony. You know what that means. We'll be all spring and maybe part of summer getting brands sorted out and the range tidied up again."

"Now that's a fact," agreed Nate. "Saw Hoot McCall in town last week and he said he'd counted better than twenty head of our cows along the stage road over by the Chinquapin Roughs. You know, Cleve, with brands scattered to hell an' gone in all directions, this range could break out in a rash of rustling. Conditions are sure made to order for it. A smart man, callin' his shots right, could make himself a real stake." Nate showed his small grin. "If I wasn't so damned lazy, I'd maybe consider that proposition myself."

"At your age!" chided Fraser. Then his tone and expression turned dry. "Rustlers don't come that smart, Nate. They just think they do. Now I never did hear of a rustler who lived to a ripe old age."

There was a stir at the door of the ranch house and Alec Cormack's tall daughter stepped out to face the morning sun. She saw Fraser immediately and lifted a graceful arm in salute, then came picking her way across the puddled earth.

Cleve Fraser had known Leslie Cormack for a long

time, yet he never saw her but that he was stirred by a small, marveling moment. For never had he known anyone who so completely reflected his environment. In this girl was a strong land's fresh vitality, the fire of its brighter moods, the strength and patience to resist its sterner ones. The warmth of its sun lay in her hair and the clear vigor of its clean winds shone in her eyes.

She was dressed for riding in a divided skirt of forest-green twill and a gray woolen blouse under a snugly buttoned jacket of smoke-cured buckskin. There was a silk muffler about her throat, and her fair hair was tucked up under a flatcrowned sombrero. She was pulling on a pair of fringed gauntlet gloves, and Fraser saw the glint of Vance Ogden's ring on her left hand.

Her naturally fresh color deepened slightly and she spoke, half-smiling. "The man stares and stares."

Fraser grinned and shrugged. "Don't blame me, Les. After a steady diet of myself and four winter-soured punchers, well—!"

She loosed the sorrel's reins and stepped smoothly into the saddle. "I was wondering if you'd forgotten how to ride, Cleve. How long since you last stopped by? At least two months ago. Don't tell me a little snow had you buffaloed that bad."

"A little snow! Girl, you don't know what you're talking about. I can show you drifts up in the Sentinels twenty feet deep."

Nate Lyons, finished with the hitching of the buckboard team, climbed into the rig to drive over to the ranch house. Leslie Cormack called after him. "Tell Mother and Dad I'm going ahead with Cleve."

She swung the sorrel around, and Fraser's dun was hard put to keep up with the first exuberant run. When she finally had her mount reined back to a jog, Leslie said, "You don't lie worth shucks, my friend. There may be twenty-foot drifts back in the mountains, but nothing of the sort around Saber."

The run had put a strong glow in her cheeks and her eyes flashed their boundless vitality. Fraser's glance went slightly somber. He said briefly, "Three's a crowd. Nothing truer than that, Les."

"Oh, nonsense!" she retorted. "I was afraid you'd say something silly like that. Three wasn't a crowd a year ago, five years ago. You and Vance and I used to have lots of good times together, mister."

"That was a year ago—five years ago," said Fraser carefully. "Things are a lot different now."

"Different—how?"

Fraser twisted up a cigarette. "Wasn't any ring on your finger then, Les. You were as free and happy as any other maverick, wearing no man's brand."

She swung her glance at him, suddenly quiet. The scarred side of his face was toward her, with its hint of taciturn harshness. She reached over and laid an impulsive hand on his arm.

"You can make me very unhappy, Cleve, if you let that ring affect our long and good friendship in any way. And I know Vance feels exactly the same."

Fraser shook himself, showed her a slightly twisted grin. "Sorry, Les. I'm a surly brute. I'll always be around when I'm wanted. Nothing means more to me than to see you happy."

They had come to a down-running ridge from the north. The road cut around the point of this and beyond stretched the sweeping miles of Bunch Grass Basin. It was a great triangle of country, the apex angling back north and east to the very flank of the curving Sentinel Mountains which, dark with timber along the lower and middle reaches, finally drove white shoulders bursting through, which seemed to float like distant cloud masses against the morning's pure sky.

Here was a stretch of country that had been a military reservation. Once troops of the United States Cavalry had patrolled these miles in the days when Indian threat lay raw and real across the land. But long since were the Indians and the troopers gone, and the barracks of the post on Red Bank Creek were abandoned.

Cattle bearing many brands had grazed across the basin, for as government land it had been free grass. But now the government was about to sell the basin at public auction to the highest bidder. Before this day's sun went down these wide, free acres would have become private ones.

"It makes me queerly sad," said Leslie Cormack abruptly.

Fraser knew what she meant, and he nodded. "Nothing so free as free land. Just riding across it makes a man feel like the edges of his life reach clear out past where the sun comes up and where it goes down. Things are going to be a lot different when Grat Mallory owns all this."

She gave a quick, disturbed sigh. "You talk just like Vance does. So certain Mallory will get it."

"Tell me who's to stop him, and how?"

"He won't be the only one to bid."

"Sure," agreed Fraser. "I know that. Your father will make his try and so will Pete Jackson and Art Wilcoxon and Dab Shurtleff. Oh, they'll all be in at the start. But it's the final bid that'll buy Bunch Grass, and that bid will be Grat Mallory's."

She looked at him slantingly. "Won't you be there?"

"As a spectator, that's all. I never waste energy reaching for shadows or something I can't touch. No profit in that, Les."

She considered a moment, a slight shadow darkening her eyes. "Grat Mallory must have made money awful fast. I can remember when he first moved in on this range, buying up the old Tanner place. He struck me as pretty skimpy stuff then. Now, of a sudden, you picture him as being entirely too prosperous for anyone to handle."

"My lovely playmate, you're overlooking something," drawled Fraser. "Which is that Grat Mallory is a sharp hombre, oh, a very sharp hombre indeed. He's organized himself a cattle company of some kind, with outside money behind him. And friend Grat isn't the kind to sit into any game unless he's got the most chips and is holding the high cards. He's holding them now, and—"

He broke off and reined in, his glance studying the moisture-darkened earth now beginning to steam faintly under the building warmth of the sun. Leslie, startled by his sudden action, jibed mischievously.

"The earth—the good, fat earth. Did you just discover it?"

The corners of Fraser's eyes pinched sharply. "Cattle been through here," he said tersely. "And horses—two horses."

He straightened, and his glance ran down the far reaches of the basin toward the Sentinels. He spoke without turning his head.

"You scatter along, Les. I'll catch up in a mile or so."

Before she could answer he'd spurred away toward the northeast, following the sign. He kept to it for a good half-mile before, satisfied with his findings, he turned, lifted the dun to a run, and angled down the distance to drop in again beside Leslie Cormack. A full two miles behind them Alec Cormack and his wife came on in the buckboard at a spanking trot.

"Fine companion you are to pick for a ride," scolded Les, smiling. "Too bad it isn't later season and the grasshoppers out. You could have yourself just a dandy time chasing them."

Fraser grinned. "I can remember when we both chased them. And used 'em for bait when we fished in Stony Creek. Those were great days, Les. Not a blessed thing on our minds but sunshine."

"And now we're old and got troubles, is that it?"

"So Soddy Joens swears," chuckled Fraser. "Soddy says folks are born to have troubles."

"Soddy's favorite color is indigo. But now you're jumping in circles again. Come on, tell sister. What did you find on your little ride?"

"Maybe a dozen head of cattle went that way, with two riders chousing them. Straight back into the Sentinels."

"And that is strange?"

"Yeah," nodded Fraser dryly. "Considering conditions and the time of years, it sure is."

"I know," she conceded gravely. "Dad was talking about that very possibility last night at supper, and hoping it wouldn't show or lead to anything drastic."

"Playing fast and loose with another man's cattle always leads to something drastic," said Fraser. "But those who play that sort of game know what the penalty can be. So they can't kick if it catches up with them."

She flashed him a swift glance. "Should you do the catching up with, I wonder would you be as tough as you sound?"

"That," evaded Fraser, "is a leading question and represents the kind of bridge I never cross until I come up with it."

Les pondered her question in silence. There were times when she felt she knew this man thoroughly. But at other times she wasn't so sure. She knew he had the capacity for fun and laughter and broad good humor, but there had been a few times back across the years when she'd seen him aroused, when his eyes would smoke up and turn dark, and utter bleakness would sweep his face. Then she could recognize a ruthlessness that was iron hard and unforgiving. Yet the man was openhanded, generous, and without a trace of meanness in him.

Quite candidly, on more than one occasion, she had asked herself what attraction it was that Vance Ogden held for her that this man did not. She knew that in many ways where Vance was weak Cleve Fraser was strong. Even back in their youthful years it was Cleve who did things, while Vance would laugh and joke and side-step.

Perhaps, she mused, knowing no trace of irresponsibility herself, it was this very thing in Vance that had drawn her. Or, she considered wryly, what some might call evidence of the maternal instinct. In any event, she was not the sort to give her heart lightly, and she had given it to Vance Ogden.

As evidence, it was his ring which she wore on her finger. And she knew that the wearing of it had made a difference in the old carefree comradeship with Cleve Fraser.

Traveling steadily, they had cut the miles down, and now the road dropped below the level of Bunch Grass and came to where the benchland slanted steeply and lost itself in a sage desert's empty grayness.

Here also, where it could serve both the high country and the low, lay the town of Mineral, its buildings a ragged spread on either side of a wide and carelessly laid-out street. Smoke winnowed pale and blue from chimney tops and windowpanes threw back the sun in bright flashes.

As they put their horses to the final drop, Fraser drawled, "After considerable time away from it, I always expect it to look better than it does. And then I always find it just the same old town, all spraddled out and homely as sin. Only one thing I know that's always up to expectations and never disappoints me."

He looked at his companion as he said this and chuckled at the swift beat of color in her cheeks. "As long as I can make you blush that way, Les, I'll always know there's one small corner of your heart that Vance Ogden doesn't own."

She tossed her head. "My friend, you presume."

When they turned in at the end of the street, they saw Vance Ogden and Henry Poe taking the sun on the edge of the porch of Poe's store. Vance, a slender, carelessly graceful man, inclined a handsome head as they rode up.

"Beauty and the beast, Henry," he drawled lazily. "How do you suppose she managed to lure him down out of the sticks?"

Then Vance was off the porch, ducking under the hitch rail and gripping Fraser's hand. "Cleve! It's good to see you. But you stay away from your friends too long."

Liking this man and showing it, Fraser grinned. "The little animals are smart, Vance. When the snow piles thick they crawl into a hole and stay there. I figured it a good example to follow."

Vance Ogden's features were cleanly chiseled and his hair showed curly and tawny as ripe wheat as he took off his hat and turned to Leslie Cormack. He was jaunty, and carried himself with a flair that made his every move smooth and effortless. He spoke across his shoulder.

"Don't mind you riding to town with my best girl, Cleve. But from here on I take over."

He held up his hand to Les who, as she took it and dismounted, gave him a smile that was warm and sweet. They moved off along the street, a handsome pair. Fraser watched them for a moment, then turned, dragging his spurs across the porch and thumbing at a pocket.

"List of grub here, Henry. Lot of airtights and sweet

20

stuff in it. Out at the ranch the boys have been fighting rough fare so much they're turning Siwash on me."

Henry Poe nodded, gave the list a brief glance, then let his eyes swing to follow Leslie Cormack and Vance Ogden.

"Think a lot of those two, don't you, Cleve?"

"Of course. We more or less grew up together."

"She's a grand girl," said Poe. "I hope she'll never be sorry."

A ripple ran across Fraser's jaw, pulling it up long and hard. His voice went slightly rough. "Damn a gossip, Henry. You've said both too much and too little. What in hell are you driving at?"

The storekeeper laid his level glance on Fraser. "I've watched my share of men, and I've seen some of them grow and some of them shrivel. Vance is a likable cuss, a pleasant man to be around. But he's got one damn bad habit."

"Name it," rapped Fraser.

"Poker, Cleve."

Fraser's laugh was brittle, without mirth. "What the devil! You can't damn a man for turning an occasional card, Henry."

"No," agreed Poe, "you can't. But Vance doesn't turn just an occasional one. He's been turning them all winter and with such poor success he's begun borrowing from his friends. Why do you think he was holding down my porch this morning? Not because the sun was shining for a change. But to talk up another loan, the third in the past ten days."

Fraser was completely still, his eyes pinching down at

the corners. "Any man can find himself in need of a few dollars."

"Three hundred isn't a few, Cleve—not when used to play poker with. Get me right. I'm no gossip, and I'm not crying about the money. But the Cormacks are my old and valued friends. I think as much of Les as I would a daughter of my own. You're my friend and so is Vance. I'm talking because I don't want anybody hurt. You've always been able to handle Vance. Get hold of him, Cleve, and shake some sense into him"

Poe would have turned into his store, but Fraser dropped a hand on his arm.

"Sorry I got wringy, Henry. Should have known you'd do only what you believed right. I'm glad you spoke up. Who with and where has Vance been doing most of his poker playing?"

"In the High Front with Grat Mallory, Breshear, Scarlett, and a couple of others of Mallory's crew. I'm not the only one to notice it. Stack Portland knows, and doesn't like it at all, for he holds a couple of Vance's notes. A little poker, Cleve, never hurt any man, but too much of it can pull him apart."

Saying this, Henry Poe went inside. Fraser stayed where he was, staring at the street, mechanically twisting up a cigarette. He was still there, the cigarette a dead butt on his lip, when Alec and Sarah Cormack came rolling into town in the buckboard.

2. Conflict Acres

THE GOVERNMENT LAND AGENT WAS NAMED STYLES, A short, brisk man. He wasted little time in getting at the business which had brought him across the desert to Mineral. Burt Statler, who knew Styles, had offered his law office as a place in which to hold the sale, and at this moment it was pretty well crowded.

Alec Cormack was there, rawboned, bluff-jawed, ruddy of cheek, with blue eyes glinting under shaggy brows that had begun to frost up with a touch of grizzle. Art Wilcoxon, lean and spare and soldier straight, was on hand. Dab Shurtleff had taken over one of the few chairs and filled it with his slightly paunchy bulk, a cigar sending curling smoke up past his blocky face. Pete Jackson, frowsy and untidy and with runover boots, squatted against a far wall, and alongside of him was Jim Lear, with his pointed, foxy face, his shriveled leatheriness, and his acid, cantankerous tongue.

Heading for Statler's office, Cleve Fraser saw Stack Portland come out of his bank and hurry that way. Fraser quickened his stride. If Stack Portland had decided to sit into this thing to the limit Grat Mallory would have a stiff fight on his hands. As Fraser reached Statler's door, Vance Ogden came angling across from the hotel. He grinned.

"You and me got as much right sitting in on this as we would to try and run for governor, Cleve."

"Always fun to look and listen," Fraser said briefly.

They went in and stood against the wall to the left of

the door. On the far side of the portal Grat Mallory had a shoulder point against the wall, watching proceedings with a shade of amusement on his smooth, dark face. He had the look of a man enjoying some secret joke all his own. He seemed unworried and supremely confident, as though this deal was already his, signed, sealed, and delivered. On the floor between his feet was a satchel of scuffed leather.

When Fraser went in he felt Mallory's glance, and he swung his head to meet it, seeing in this man someone he did not like and never could. Physically, Mallory was big and rugged enough, and not a bad-looking man. His hair was dark, his features balanced and without blemish. His eyes were black and had a trick of going blank and veiled and completely unreadable when under hard scrutiny. There was a smoothness about him which Fraser bluntly catalogued as slick. A man might guess at what was going on in Mallory's mind, but he could never be sure.

Styles, the land agent, glanced at his watch, then droned through a copy of the posted-sale announcement. That done with, he laid the paper down and looked around.

"The sale is open, gentlemen. Give me a bid."

"Ten thousand," was Alec Cormack's prompt reply.

"Eleven," said Art Wilcoxon quietly.

"Twelve," came back Cormack.

Dab Shurtleff took his cigar from his heavy lips, surveyed it gravely, then grunted. "Fifteen."

Pete Jackson cleared his throat harshly, seemed about to speak, but instead gnawed a corner off a plug of tobacco and stared at the floor. Pete was a cautious man with money; it hurt him to spend any of it, even for the rarest kind of bargain. Apparently he had already decided that the pace was going to be entirely too stiff for him.

Art Wilcoxon, seeing that Jackson wasn't getting in, said, "Sixteen thousand."

Dab Shurtleff sagged a little deeper into his chair and shrugged his beefy shoulders. "Sixteen five."

"Seventeen," growled Alec Cormack.

There was a slight pause, the room going quiet. Styles looked around inquiringly. So far Grat Mallory hadn't said a word. But now he made his first bid, and he hiked things stiffly. "Twenty thousand."

Alec Cormack and Art Wilcoxon both threw measuring glances at Mallory. So did white haired Stack Portland who, standing at Alec Cormack's shoulder, had been completely silent. Mallory met the glances with slightly crinkled black eyes. Mallory was enjoying this.

"Twenty-one thousand," said Art Wilcoxon, with a lingering reluctance. Wilcoxon was getting close to his limit. "Twenty-two," rumbled Alec Cormack, bristling.

Now Dab Shurtleff surprised. "Twenty-three," he said grimly.

Grat Mallory took over with another bold jump. "Twenty-five."

Art Wilcoxon made a hard, cutting motion with his hand and said disgustedly, "Hell with it!" He turned and walked out. Now it was between Alec Cormack, Dab Shurtleff, and Grat Mallory, with Stack Portland still silent.

"Twenty-six thousand," gritted Dab Shurtleff.

"Twenty-six five," said Alec Cormack stubbornly.

Dab Shurtleff threw the chewed butt of his cigar into a corner. "All right, Alec. Mallory is all your cat now. See if you can skin him."

"Tough chore, Shurtleff," mocked Mallory. "Twenty-seven thousand."

Watching closely, Cleve Fraser saw hesitation and doubt take hold of Alec Cormack, saw a shadow of weariness pull at his face. And he did not miss the smug glitter in Mallory's eyes.

"I can scrape up maybe ten thousand, Alec," Fraser offered. "It's yours if you want it. Stay with him!"

Mallory's lounging shoulder came away from the wall and he half-turned, his voice lashing thin across the room.

"This is a man's game, Fraser. Pikers stay out!"

Fraser's eyes began to smoke up and darken. "Don't get too proud all at once, Mallory. Well, Alec?"

Cormack shook his head. "Good of you, Cleve, but I'll play it this way."

Styles, the government man, spoke up. "Twenty-seven thousand I'm bid."

Alec Cormack looked at Stack Portland, who nodded. "Twenty-eight," said Cormack.

"Twenty-nine," rapped Mallory. He was truculent now.

Cormack sighed deeply. "Thirty thousand."

"Thirty-one," snapped Mallory.

Cormack looked at Stack Portland again, and this time Portland shook his head. Cormack said simply, "I'm done."

Styles turned to Mallory. "A cash deal, you under-stand?"

Mallory said, "Sure. I know that. And I got it—here." He caught up the leather satchel, swaggered to the desk.

Alec Cormack and Stack Portland tramped out. Fraser and Vance Ogden followed. Then came Dab Shurtleff with Pete Jackson and Jim Lear. Vance Ogden gave a light laugh. "That's the way it goes."

Fraser said nothing, darkness still smoking up his eyes. Alec Cormack and Stack Portland were on the way to Portland's bank. Dab Shurtleff looked around and said, "I've a feeling that some of us just lost our shirts. But I'll buy a drink."

They trooped over to the High Front. Art Wilcoxon was there, brooding over a whisky. As Fraser dropped in at the bar beside him, Wilcoxon tipped his head. "Hell of a note, Cleve. A johnny-come-lately like Mallory. He got it, of course?"

"He got it," answered Fraser bluntly. "But he could have been stopped."

"How? He had it in the bag. Rest of us were just punching empty air—just going through the motions."

"That's right, Art, you were. As individuals. But if you'd got together and pooled your money, you could have licked him. Instead, you were all a little greedy, trying to grab off the prize all alone. So you got nothing and Mallory got it all."

Wilcoxon stared at his glass. "Why, now, you've got something there, Cleve."

At the pool table in the rear Loop Scarlett and Chess Breshear were knocking the balls around. Observing the gloom at the bar, they both grinned. They knew which way the cat had jumped.

"Well, anyhow," said Pete Jackson, "he didn't get it for nothin'. He had to go past thirty thousand. That's a pretty fair chunk of money."

"He didn't have to go that high because of anything you or Jim Lear did," reminded Shurtleff caustically. "Neither of you opened your yaps."

"What the hell!" grumbled Jackson. "That game was way too fast for Jim or me right from the start. And when a man can't afford to buy chips he's smart to keep his mouth shut."

"No use throwin' rocks at one another," put in Wilcoxon. "It's over and done with and Mallory's got it."

"Right!" agreed Shurtleff. "He's got it. But something tells me nothing is over and done with. This could be just the start of a lot of things."

A moody silence fell, each man considering Dab Shurtleff's words and comparing them with his own private estimate of the future. It was Vance Ogden who finally spoke in his usual careless shoulder-shrugging way. "I guess the sun will go on rising and setting, same as always."

Dab Shurtleff looked at him, a certain thinly veiled contempt in his eyes. "Sometimes that salve gets a little thick, Ogden. So far you've always managed to find a hole in the fence to crawl through. But you're due one of these days to bump into a fence without any hole in it. When you do, I'm wondering if you'll have the stuff to climb over it."

Vance flushed and tipped his drink.

The door of the High Front swung and Grat Mallory came in. He gave his satchel a slide toward the pool table. "Watch that, Chess," he ordered. "There's still plenty in it." He spun a chair from under a poker table and sat down, pushing his legs well ahead, and smiling as he lit a cigar.

"Right now," he announced loudly, "is a good time for an understanding all around. About Bunch Grass Basin. Some changes in policy are in order. Here's the first one. Starting now, every blade of grass in that basin is for Rafter X cattle, no others. I'm allowing just ten days for all other brands to get their last stray off Bunch Grass. After that time limit they'll be choused to hell an' gone, and where they end up is no concern of mine. Now here is something else. All roads and trails across any part of Bunch Grass are closed to any and everybody except Rafter X men. That means, keep off basin land. I mean—off! Is that understood?"

There was a short silence, then Dab Shurtleff swung his glance around. "See what I meant when I said nothing was over and done with?"

Cleve Fraser, his drink still untouched, pushed away from the bar and stepped out to face Mallory. There was dark smoke in his eyes and little ripples of tautness flicked the hard angle of his jaw.

"Mallory," he said softly, "I want to hear you say that again. The last part, I mean. You've bought Bunch Grass and it's yours. Up to a certain point. You can hog the grass. But the town trail from Saber and Shield and Cross cuts across the lower end of Bunch Grass. Are you trying to tell me that trail is now closed?"

Mallory's smooth, dark smile reached tauntingly through the smoke of his cigar. "Your hearing must be bad, Fraser. I couldn't have made it any plainer."

Now the room did go quiet, and a thin tension crept all across it. Back at the pool table Chess Breshear and Loop Scarlett laid aside their cues and came forward a few steps. At the bar, Art Wilcoxon caught Dab Shurtleff's eye, who nodded. So now these two turned and laid their strict attention on Breshear and Scarlett. Pete Jackson and Jim Lear eased toward the far end of the bar, an air of complete neutrality about them. Vance Ogden did not move.

Fraser paid no attention to any of this. He stood in front of Mallory, his boring glance a solid and unswerving force. Under the impact of it Mallory's smile became a set grimace, his black eyes taking on that shallow blankness. It was as though he had drawn a curtain across his mind, hiding it completely. Fraser's words came, low and brittle.

"So you think you're that big, eh, Mallory? Well now, hear this. I'll be moving back and forth along that trail to town whenever I feel like it. So will my riders. Knowing the man, it's my guess Alec Cormack will feel the same way about it. Just how do you propose to stop us?"

"I'll close the trail my own way," retorted Mallory thinly. "I'll be particularly definite with you, Fraser. I never did like the way you rode down any trail or street. Cormack's bidding for Bunch Grass was legitimate. Your piker offer to back his hand wasn't. You made it plain then that you'd like nothing better than to plant your boots on me. And when any piker takes a bite at me I got my own kind of answer for them."

"Piker, piker, piker," said Fraser, soft as the wind. "Three times you've used the word. Only my friends can call me names. Mallory, you need cutting down to size!"

Fraser took a short, quick stride. His open hand shot out, the hard palm and spread fingers framing Mallory's face, the pressure making a wreck of Mallory's cigar. Then Fraser straightened his bent elbow with a snap. Mallory and his chair went over backward, the crash a hard racket through the room.

Mallory turned almost completely over, landing on the broad of his shoulders. He spat a curse and was trying to get at his gun when Fraser kicked the chair out of the way and dropped on him. He wrestled Mallory's gun from him and sent it skittering to one side. Then he set back, jerked Mallory to his feet, and flung him against the poker table.

"Have a swing, Grat!" he invited wickedly.

Mallory let one go and Fraser took it high on a hunched left shoulder as he stepped inside and hit Mallory twice in the body, solid, smashing blows. Mallory gasped and grabbed at him. They wrestled back and forth, two big men, well matched in weight and height.

At the rear of the room Chess Breshear and Loop Scarlett split up and began sliding forward, one on either side. Art Wilcoxon flagged them down with a hard wave of his hand.

"Let be, you two!" he rapped. "This is between Cleve

and Mallory—about a trail."

"Right!" seconded Dab Shurtleff, a far more dangerous man than he looked. "About a trail. Whether it stays open or is closed. Don't try anything foolish, boys!"

In the test of sheer strength Fraser began to win an advantage, the two savage body blows having done Mallory little good. So now Mallory gave back suddenly, pulled clear, and drove a hard hook to the side of Fraser's neck. It was a shrewd blow, and it staggered Fraser. Before he could recover he took another, glancingly, across his face. It cut his lips and brought the warm seep of blood.

Sight of the crimson stain set Mallory off. He swarmed in, both fists swinging. Fraser crouched, arms about his head. He took a smash to the body and a ripping uppercut to his bruised mouth. He backed away a stride, straightened, and shot out a driving left. The punch caught Mallory coming in, snapped his head back, and set him up for the winging right that followed.

This was easily the hardest blow yet thrown. It hung Mallory on his heels, wavering and wide open. Fraser went in fast and sunk both fists into Mallory's body again, grunting with the savage effort he put behind the blows. They caught Mallory with his belly muscles flaccid and loose and hurt him wickedly. He sagged back against the poker table and nearly fell as the table skidded away from his reeling weight.

Fraser was waiting when Mallory straightened and turned. He uncoiled from his very heels, and the shock of the blow, catching Mallory fairly on his wobbling jaw, left Fraser's arm and wrist slightly numb. Mallory went down in a long sprawl, staying there, sick and retching and only half-conscious.

For a long moment Fraser stood over him, watching. Then Fraser's head came up and he put a challenging stare on Loop Scarlett and Breshear. They met the look, but that was all.

Fraser turned back to the bar and at a glance read the significance of the positions and attitudes of the men there. He nodded his thanks to Art Wilcoxon and Dab Shurtleff and said, a trifle hoarsely, "This drink is on me. Pipe, a bar towel—a clean one."

Pipe Orr, who owned the High Front and did his own bar chores, supplied the towel, and Fraser dabbed the blood from his face. He looked at Vance Ogden, saw what was behind Vance's forced grin, and said with some curtness, "If it's not there, don't try and cover it up."

Then he turned back to the bar and so did not see the dull color flame in Vance's handsome face.

The whisky stung Fraser's battered lips but took some of the raw rasp out of his throat. Art Wilcoxon called for another and lifted his glass. "To a trail kept open, Cleve. Man! You took him apart."

"Thereby reducing a hat size, we hope," growled Dab Shurtleff.

Reaction set in. Fraser downed his second drink, laid some money on the bar, and went out into the open sunlight of the street, not at all satisfied with himself. So he'd whipped Mallory in a fist swinging, but what had the brawl proven and what good had it done? It hadn't

33

reduced Mallory's power in any way, and now Mallory would hate him worse than ever and be tougher about Bunch Grass.

Fraser twisted up a cigarette, lipped it gingerly. Now that he'd begun to relax he realized he'd burned up a lot of energy in there. He let his big shoulders go slack and, as he recalled his remark to Vance Ogden, knew another gust of anger at himself.

Knowing and liking Vance, he'd long ago realized what Vance had and what he lacked. Vance had never been a fighter, not in a physical sense. His way was an easy, smiling, cheerful acceptance of life which saw no sense in beating up another man or in getting beat up himself.

Was Vance to be blamed if he hadn't been born with the raw, black physical will to invite a fight or to move into one? That was no reflection on Vance or any other man, for that matter—he couldn't help it any more than he could the color of his skin. There were far bigger things in the world than blind, dark physical courage. That sort of thing was cheap enough; some of the most surly, worthless whelps Fraser had ever met up with possessed that. It was easy not to be afraid when a man didn't know what fear was. Often had Fraser envied Vance his gay and easy charm. Maybe in the long run that sort of thing could get a man more than all the rough violence in the world.

The smoke of the cigarette was a bitter rasp across his raw lips, so in sudden distaste Fraser tossed it away, considered the street for another period of dark brooding, and was about to head for Henry Poe's store when the doors of the High Front swung and Vance Ogden came out. Fraser dropped a quick hand on Vance's arm.

"Sorry, fellah. That was a mean crack in there, and I'm taking it back."

There was a flush on Vance's face and a faintly bitter smile on his lips. "Why take it back? It's true. I haven't the nerve of a rabbit in a fight. Never did have. I'd give plenty to have some of your burly brute in me."

"Right now you can have it all," said Fraser. "I'm fed up with myself. I'll trade for the instincts of a gentleman any time."

"Forget it," said Vance. "I have."

Vance said it easy enough, but there was something in his manner to belie the words. He would have gone his way, but Fraser said, "Hold it a minute, cowboy." Then, because he knew no other way to go at a problem but by tackling it directly and with both hands, Fraser said doggedly, "You in need of money?"

Vance's faint smile grew set. "What gave you that idea?"

"This and that. If you are, come to me. Only—"

"Only—what?"

"When a man has to borrow money to pay his poker debts, he's playing too much poker. Winter's over, kid. Lot of range to ride now, lot of cows to chouse. Tell me how much you need to get squared away, and with that off the books we'll start polishing saddle leather again."

Vance's set smile faded out. He stared off at nothing, but he spoke distinctly, setting each word down sharply. "My thanks and all that sort of thing, Cleve. But there's some things in my life I don't want you prying into.

Suppose we understand that, once and for all!"

Vance pulled away from Fraser's hand and walked off.

Fraser stared after him for a space and then, in sudden disgust for the way this whole day had turned out, headed for Henry Poe's store, determined to pick up his grub order and go home. But Alec Cormack came out of Stack Portland's bank and intercepted him.

"Want you to know I appreciated your offer, Cleve. But I was already bidding against Mallory on Stack Portland's money and had no right to drag you in." Cormack's eyes narrowed. "Who hit you?"

Fraser explained briefly his set-to with Mallory. "He was pretty starchy over getting Bunch Grass and I let his talk get under my skin. Guess I made a damn fool of myself, Alec."

Cormack swung a wrathful head. "That man's got a complex, Cleve. Hell with him! We'll use the town trail same as always, and let's see him stop us. Now there's something else that Stack Portland was telling me about," went on the grizzled cattleman grimly. "Something I don't like—don't like at all."

"Yeah?" murmured Fraser. "What's that?" But he knew what it was, even as he asked.

"It's Vance. He's been playing too much poker and losing too much money at it."

"Heard some talk of that," parried Fraser cautiously. "I wouldn't worry too much about it. He'll snap out of it."

"Now he damn well better!" vowed Cormack. "I know man is a cussed poor excuse of an animal, take him by and large, so I don't expect the one who marries my daughter to be a saint. Still and all, he's got to be able to take his liquor or leave it alone. And he's got to have the brains and backbone to know when it's time to get up and walk away from a poker table. There's no place in my family for any man who can't do either or both of those two things. That includes Vance Ogden. You staying in town overnight, Cleve?"

"I'd figured to when I came in." Fraser nodded. "Now I'm not so sure. Why?"

"Sarah says you're to have supper with us at the hotel. Better not disappoint her."

Grat Mallory and his two riders, Breshear and Scarlett, came out of the High Front. Breshear had Mallory by the elbow, steadying him, while Scarlett carried Mallory's leather satchel. Mallory shook off Breshear's aiding hand and climbed into his saddle, needing a distinct effort to do so. As they came down the street at a jog Breshear and Scarlett showed only a wary surliness, but Mallory, face bruised and swollen, eyelids puffed, laid a glance on Cleve Fraser that was ophidian and glittering.

"You definitely mussed him up, Cleve," observed Cormack. "Now he'll hate you clear past hell."

"That," said Fraser dryly, "I can stand. But his friendship would wither me."

Cormack studied Fraser gravely. "I've known you ever since you were a lanky kid, yet at times I don't completely understand you. Like today. Bunch Grass Basin means less to you, actually, than to any of the rest of us. You've never grazed cattle on it to any extent, nor your father before you. Your range is all well west and higher up. So you've really no heavy cause to quarrel with Mallory. Yet when the bidding was going on you stood willing to back me to your full limit. And just now you let some gas out of Mallory's balloon over in the High Front. I wonder about those things."

Fraser teetered back and forth from heel to toe, considering. "Some men, like toadstools, grow in dark corners and feed on superior matter, Alec. Mallory strikes me as that sort. Put it down that I just don't like the man. We ruffed feathers at each other the first time we ever met. I guess it will always be that way."

"Well," said Cormack, "when you clouted him you did something I'd like to have done myself. The man's come along awful fast, and there's a smugness in him. He's got power behind him somewhere. I wish I knew where, and how much."

"That, I think, we'll find out in time," Fraser said.

On the porch of the Timberline Hotel, which stood at the far end of the street, Mrs. Cormack appeared and waved a beckoning arm. Alec Cormack started off.

"There's Sarah, calling me for something. Don't forget about supper, Cleve. You're expected."

Came noon, Fraser sauntered out to a long, low building at the edge of town where he was welcomed by one Pio Cardenas, who was leathery dark with merry eyes. Savory odors drifted from an open door. Fraser said, "I've fed on ranch grub all winter, Pio, until it all tastes like sawdust. I've a hunger for something hot and full of bite to bring my appetite back."

Pio's eyes twinkled. "You are just in time, *amigo*. My Maria but now is putting it on the table."

Over past years Fraser had eaten with these good people many times, for they were friends of long standing. Short like her spouse, but considerably broader, Maria Cardenas knew kindliness equal to her bulk. There was also a daughter, Teresa, plainly the magnet which had drawn young Danny Cope to this same generous table.

Danny Cope was a yellow-headed, reckless, devil-may-care kid who had, at one time or another, drawn wages from nearly every outfit in the Sentinel country. He hailed Fraser cheerfully.

"When you set out to curry a short horse, Cleve, why don't you spread the word first, so a man could be there and see the fun?"

"Sometimes the idea hits all of a sudden, Danny," answered Fraser dryly. "And it wasn't all fun." He touched a finger to his cut lips. "Who you signing on with, kid, for spring round-up?"

Danny shrugged carelessly. "Hadn't thought about it yet."

"When you find time, how about giving Saber a tumble? I'll guarantee to work some of the salt out of you."

Danny grinned. "That I well know."

The meal over, Fraser and Pio Cardenas went in to the Tatter's workshop at the far end of the building. Here, in a room cluttered with saddles, riatas, headstalls, and all manner of leather goods, Pio's nimble fingers performed magic with awl and wax end. Men saved wages carefully and rode long distances to buy items of equipment from Pio Cardenas. And because Pio was a good and shrewd listener, there was no better place to glean little items of range news than right here in this shop.

Fraser, musing over a cigarette, observed gravely, "Been a pretty tough winter, Pio. Brands scattered everywhere. Now if I had ideas about the other fellow's cattle, I'd figure the setup as just right. It's an idea some may be playing with."

Pio, already at work at his bench, ducked a round head. "Some men are that way, Señor Cleve. And it is very bad business."

"You hear things," went on Fraser, "and you see things. Small things, maybe, yet things that tell a big story sometimes. And from time to time you and me have little talks together. That is true, isn't it?"

Gray eyes and black ones met in understanding. Pio nodded again. Fraser smiled grimly and moved to the door. "Your Maria is a wonderful cook, Pio. Thank her for me."

Back again on the street, Fraser dropped into the High Front, looking for Vance Ogden, for the uncomfortable note on which they had parted still nagged him. But the High Front was empty except for Pipe Orr behind the bar and Art Wilcoxon playing solitaire at a poker table. Pipe Orr reported that Vance had been in again, just before noon, and had said something about heading out for home. Which news troubled Fraser more than ever.

For he knew that behind Leslie Cormack's visit to town had been the eagerness to see Vance. Now, if Vance had pulled out it would be because of the remarks Fraser had made with the harsh fires of anger burning in him. So he'd hurt Les Cormack as well as Vance. He looked across the bar.

"Temper, Pipe," he said morosely, "can make the damnedest fool of a man."

He bought a cigar then went over and pulled out a chair across from Art Wilcoxon. "Where's Shurtleff and Jackson and Lear, Art?"

Wilcoxon grunted. "Headed out. I tried to drum up a little game of draw, but no go. Jackson and Lear in particular seemed worried about their stock, saying the winter had scattered them from hell to breakfast."

"Reminds me," murmured Fraser. "Saw some sign when I was coming in across Bunch Grass this morning."

Wilcoxon quit shoving the cards around and his head lifted. "Yeah?"

"Yeah. Maybe a dozen or fifteen head of critters, with two riders chousing them. I ran the sign down a ways to make sure where it headed. It lined straight for the upper end of Bunch Grass."

Wilcoxon scrubbed his chin with thumb and forefinger. "The direction is all sour, Cleve. Now if they'd been bringing the cattle this way, toward lower range, where they'd be handy to pick up in roundup, it would have made sense. As it was—"

"You got it, Art. We're going to have our troubles this year, I'm afraid."

Wilcoxon's face went harsh. "They will try it, won't they? The damn fools! Risk their necks against a rope just for a few head of critters. Well, should I come up with any of them, they'll get what they're asking for."

Fraser touched a fresh match to his cigar. "Good of

you and Shurtleff to keep Breshear and Scarlett off my neck a while ago. Appreciate it."

Wilcoxon snorted. "Think nothing of it. Mallory had just announced the rules, hadn't he? Him against the world. Well, if that's the way he wants it, that's the way it'll be."

3. Grim Portent

AT A LITTLE PAST MIDAFTERNOON HOOT MCCALL brought the stage from Canyon City swaying into town behind a lathered team of six. He hauled up in front of the hotel and while Jerry Pine and a couple of hostlers led the tired team away and brought up a fresh one from Jerry's stable, Hoot went into the hotel for a bait of grub.

When the stage was ready to roll again on its next leg of the route across the desert to rail's end at Breed's Junction, Henry Poe carried a slim mailbag over for Hoot to stow in the front boot. Styles, the government land agent, done with the chore that had brought him to Mineral, came out of the hotel and climbed into the stage, carrying a well-stuffed and soundly locked brief case. Hoot McCall hitched his gaunt lankiness up to the box and the Concord rumbled down street and turned into the desert, leather thorough braces sending back their dry, complaining creak.

Cleve Fraser killed considerable time in Payette's barbershop, emerging finally with a haircut and with lips reduced of much of their swelling by a series of hot-towel compresses. He had now decided to make a night of it in town and take up the supper invitation with the Cormack family.

At this early season of the year day shortened sharply, once the sun began to dip, and winter's lingering chill made itself felt. Fraser stood on the porch of Henry Poe's store and watched a bearded squatter from over in the Heckleman Ford country hurriedly load up some supplies and then urge his spring-wagon team out of town at a ponderous trot. Measuring distance against day's hastening end, Fraser knew the man was in for a cold, dark ride before reaching the comfort of his own fireside. If it was comfort, in some fragile lath-and-tarpaper shanty.

Knowing what the impact of winter had been on people living behind far stouter walls, Fraser could guess at the hardships the squatter and his family had faced in the months past. And he marveled at the courage and sheer tenacity of such folk. There had to be, he mused, a deathless love of the earth to hold them to their poor acres and frugal dwellings.

Behind him, Henry Poe closed the store door against the bite of the wind now beginning to sweep down from the snowy, frigid heights of the distant Sentinels. Day's temporary warmth was completely gone now. Come morning and there would be ice in the muddy ruts of the street.

Earlier, Fraser had taken both his dun and Leslie Cormack's sorrel mount over to Jerry Pine's stable. Now he went over there to give both animals a currying and see that they were well bedded for a cold night. Gloom deepened in the stable, and when Fraser came out into the street again, it was to face a chill blue dusk.

Miles out in the desert Hoot McCall got into an ankle-long, sheepskin-lined canvas coat, wrapped a ragged old muffler around his neck and ears, and settled back to stoic it out to Breed's junction, which was a long five hours away. Hoot had been at this sort of thing for the best part of his life, and the worst of winter's biting cold and summer's blasting heat had turned him leathery and tough and built up in him a vast capacity for gruff and uncomplaining silence.

On all sides the desert ran away, black and empty, trapped by the down-pressing cone of the heavens, with the stars beginning to glitter frostily through a high-forming haze. The earth's moist dankness pushed odors up, and the warm breath of the steadily traveling team washed back to Hoot, bringing its own comfort to a man who had lived all his life with horses. The road had its rough spots, but it was comparatively straight all the way to Breed's junction, and the wise and willing team could be depended upon virtually to drive itself. So Hoot let his faculties drop far back, and he stole a few moments of dozing every now and then.

He was jerked out of one of these periods when the even cadence of the team's travel broke sharply, the leaders rearing back and blocking the balance of the team. Hoot, wide awake on the instant, peered ahead into the blackness.

He saw the round bloom of gun flame and felt the smash of the bullet at the same instant. The slug hit him in the left shoulder high up, and the impact swayed him back and toppled him across the box, from where, dazed and sick, he slid down to huddle on the footboard.

Figures, only the vaguest of shadows against the earth's cold blackness, closed in on either side of the stage, yanking open the doors. Styles, the government land agent and sole passenger, jerked from uneasy drowse, had stout stuff in him. He had a gun in a shoulder holster and he went for it, for he was a faithful man, and there was thirty-one thousand dollars of government money in that brief case of his.

But Styles was stiff and clumsy with the cold and he had on an overcoat, tightly buttoned. Before he could get at his weapon an exploring hand had settled on his ankle. A savage pull hauled him half off the seat. He tried to kick free, found that he couldn't, so dived at the owner of that tenacious hand. He went through the stage door cleanly, crashing into someone who staggered back, cursing.

Styles was free, but the impetus of his gallant try had him off balance and he landed on his hands and knees on the cold, dark earth beside the stage. He was still in that position when a man stood over him and savagely pumped three heavy six-gun slugs into him. Styles flattened down and never stirred again. So died a brave man out in that chill and lonely desert.

The man who had done the shooting stepped past Styles's still figure and fumbled around in the stage's dark interior. He located the brief case, lifted it out, and his voice sounded, low and harsh, against the almost breathless silence that had closed in after the hard roll of smashing gun reports.

"I got it. Now let's get out of here!"

Hoot McCall had never gone completely out. As

though from some great distance he was conscious of the brief flurry of action in and around the stage, of the three hammering shots, and of a few indistinct, growled words. After that came the fading mutter of hoofs, and then was left only the silence and the cold.

When the shock of his wound began to wear off slightly, the grim old stage whip stirred and managed to get back to his seat, where he hunched dizzily. Remembering something, he pawed around with his sound hand and from under a corner of the folded blankets which made his seat cushion brought out a pint whisky bottle, half full. He held the bottle between his knees, pulled the cork, and took a deep drag. The whisky bit in, warming him and driving away the fuzz that clung to his senses. He corked the bottle and put it in the deep side pocket of his long coat. A measure of strength began to return.

He thrust his right hand inside his coat and explored his wounded shoulder. There was warm and sticky blood in there, but it did not seem too bad, though his whole arm and shoulder was weak and useless and now began to set up a throbbing ache. It could, thought Hoot bleakly, have been a lot worse.

Remembering his passenger he turned, leaned slightly over, and sent a harsh call. "How's it down there?"

There was no answer. Hoot went down off the stage very carefully. Reaching the ground, he did not take two steps before he stumbled over the body of Styles. Hoot dropped to one knee and ran his hand over the still figure. Touch was enough. This man was dead.

Hoot remembered that his passenger had carried a brief case with him when he got into the stage back at

Mineral, so now Hoot explored the stage's interior for that. It wasn't there, so the picture was clear. He had, Hoot figured, the answer to the holdup. Now what to do?

Hoot measured time and distance, his own condition, and a number of other factors. Though he was considerable distance out from Mineral it was still a shorter stretch back to town than it was out ahead to Breed's Junction. And with only one good hand to work with, and weakened down as he was from his own wound, Hoot knew he had no chance of getting Styles back into the stage.

Hoot McCall's mind ran in simple, uncomplicated channels. And he had his own code of ethics, which weren't at all complicated, either. As Hoot saw it, it simply wouldn't be decent to drive on and leave that dead man there. Yet he couldn't stay here until someone came along, for that might well be a matter of days, as there was little travel along this stretch of lonely desert road except by his own stage and an occasional freighter, hauling in supplies to Mineral. Besides, he himself had only so much strength left. That wounded shoulder was really beginning to punish him. Sticking close to hard logic, Hoot knew what he must do. He had to get back to Mineral.

This was the hungry season here in the desert, and at the fag end of a hard winter. Without the stage around the coyotes would not be long in finding the body of Styles. But with the stage standing by, that would serve to hold them off. So, Hoot concluded, his move was to break a horse out of the team and ride it back.

He climbed painfully back to the box, set the brake up hard. Of the team he decided one of the wheelers would probably be the steadiest and least inclined to pitch with him. So he cut out the near one of these. It was a slow and painful business, working in the dark and with only one hand.

The horse, a big solid bay, had been ridden before and showed no tendency to pitch, much to Hoot's great relief. The animal was willing enough, and moved out at a very respectable jog. Again Hoot measured time and distance against his own capacity to endure, plus the amount of whisky left in the flask. It all added up to a pretty tight finish. Hoot closed his mind into a narrow groove of determination and rode the night down.

Jonas Cain and his wife, Abbie, took pride in setting a good table in the dining room of their Timberline Hotel. As a rule, diners ate off tables covered with spotlessly clean oilcloth, but when she wanted to, and felt that the occasion warranted such, then Abbie Cain could spread one of those tables with real linen napery and lay it with fine ware and cutlery.

Being a long-time friend and confidant of Sarah Cormack, Abbie Cain had done herself proud this evening. So when Cleve Fraser clanked down the length of the dining room to the Cormack table, he showed the dismay he felt.

"Pretty rich fare for a cowhand just down out of the timber," he exclaimed. "Mother Cormack, this looks like an occasion."

Sarah Cormack shook her head, smiling. "Nothing

special, Cleve. Just Abbie Cain showing off a bit. Sit you down and relax, boy. You'll do fully as well as Alec."

Alec Cormack grunted. "Abbie means well, but I wish she'd left out the extra fork. Always tangles me up."

There had been an extra place set, and Fraser glanced at it.

"I'd hoped to have Vance with us," said Sarah Cormack. "But he must have had other business. I wanted to see the five of us around the same table again. So often I think back to the days when Leslie and you two boys, fresh from some helter-skelter ride, would come charging into the ranch house, to raid my kitchen like ravenous young wolves."

"Good days, Mother Cormack." Fraser nodded. "The best."

Sitting across from Leslie, Fraser saw that though she was faintly smiling and seemed easy and composed, there was a shadow in her eyes. That empty seat beside her . . .

She was a brave girl, never one to inflict her own troubled thoughts on others. Under the lamplight her hair took on an almost ruddy shine, and the cast of her head and shoulders was very fine. This girl, he thought, would manage a smile through any misery, and he paid her tribute with a steady, admiring glance. That she understood his thought he was certain, for she was always mentally alert and responsive to such things. He did not mind when she took refuge in a gentle jibing.

"You recover quickly, Cleve. Dad said it would be days before Grat Mallory looked normal. You show hardly any signs."

Fraser grinned. "If that's really so, thank Frenchy Payette. Used up nearly every towel in his barbershop, putting on compresses. Oh, I stopped a few with my face, all right."

"Brawling in a saloon," she teased. "Aren't you ashamed?"

"Now, Leslie," said Mother Cormack, "don't you pick at Cleve. I'm sure he had good reason to whip Mallory."

"Hah!" growled Alec Cormack. "Any reason is good enough for that. Cleve only did what a lot of us would like to do."

"Alec was telling me about Mallory's threat to block our trail to town," Mother Cormack said. "Do you think he really meant that, Cleve?"

Fraser nodded. "Maybe. He's drunk with his own importance."

"If he does try it, what will you do?" asked Leslie. "Wait! I'll bet I know. You'll use it anyhow."

"You could be right," Fraser admitted. Then he added, grinning, "How'd you guess?"

"Didn't have to guess. I know you, my friend. There's a broad stubborn streak in you. Bullheaded is another word for it. Like the time you wouldn't take me to the dance out at the old army post, when you knew I was dying to go. And why wouldn't you? Just because you knew the Lockyears were going to be there."

"In which," declared Mother Cormack, "Cleve showed better judgment than you, my dear, the Lockyears being the sort they are. They could have made trouble."

"Little Clevie wasn't afraid of trouble, Mother,

because once before he licked that Lockyear pair. No, he was just being perverse."

"I declare!" exclaimed Mother Cormack spiritedly. "You're the one who is being perverse, Les. Leave the boy alone, so he can eat in peace."

Talk drifted into other channels, and though Leslie managed to get in several more verbal jabs at Fraser, he enjoyed his meal thoroughly. When they got up to leave, Leslie dropped in beside him, tucked her hand into his, and murmured an apology.

"Sorry I was ornery, Cleve. But I just had to snap at somebody. He—he might have stayed in town long enough to eat with us."

Looking down at her, Fraser understood completely. There was just the faintest quiver of hurt on her lips. "Any old time it'll make you feel better, Les, you just go ahead and spur me," he told her. "I won't mind a bit."

Her slim fingers tightened about his before she withdrew them, and she showed him the old brave smile again.

In the hotel parlor Leslie and her mother and Abbie Cain drifted off together. Fraser talked with Alec Cormack and Jonas Cain for a while, bought cigars at the hotel bar, then went out. The night air hit him like a thin-edged knife. Overhead the stars were frosty. Fraser hurried his stride to the High Front, where he spent a comfortable evening playing three-handed cutthroat with Art Wilcoxon and Jerry Pine. When the ancient clock over Pipe Orr's bar bonged out eleven measured notes, Fraser went back to the now-silent hotel, sought his room, and turned in.

He awoke in the cold dark, with Art Wilcoxon shaking his shoulder. Wilcoxon said curtly, "Come down to Jerry Pine's stable, Cleve," then hurried out without any further explanation.

Ice crunched under Fraser's boot heels in the ruts of the street. There was lantern light showing in Jerry Pine's harness room and the biting smell of iodoform was in the air. Doc Curtain was in there with Art Wilcoxon and Jerry Pine. Doc was working over someone on the wall bunk.

Fraser pushed in for a look. It was Hoot McCall, his leathery face pinched and seamed. Doc was bandaging Hoot's left shoulder. Art Wilcoxon moved over to the small stove in the corner and freshened the fire in it. Fraser asked, "What is this?"

"Hoot was held up out in the desert," explained Jerry Pine. "He woke me up a little while ago when he stumbled in here, half-frozen and out on his feet."

The bucket of water on the stove began to steam. Doc Curtain said, "Fill a glass half full of whisky, Art, and the rest with that hot water. There's a full pint in my bag."

They propped Hoot up and poured the hot drink into him. He groaned and opened his eyes. "Don't waste words, Hoot," ordered Doc. "But give us the story."

Hoot gave it, haltingly, then, under the influence of the drink and growing warmth, inside and out, plus his own weakness, sagged down and began to doze. Doc Curtain heaped blankets over him and said gruffly, "Tough old codger and a damned good man. He'll be all right."

Art Wilcoxon said bleakly, "Murder and robbery. That

fellow Styles had thirty-one thousand dollars with him. This is rough business. Feel like a ride, Cleve?"

"Right with you." Fraser nodded briefly.

"The stage has got to go through to Breed's junction," said Jerry Pine. "I'll drive it. I'll take along a spare wheeler."

It was a cold and bitter ride, chasing down the long miles in these black, early-morning hours. Day was breaking grayly across the world when they reached the scene of the holdup. Everything was just as Hoot McCall left it, except that the five remaining horses of the team had swung around and bunched up in a mutual move against the cold. They straightened out the team and hitched in the wheeler Jerry Pine had brought along. They lifted the stiffened figure of Styles into the stage and then Jerry climbed to the box and kicked off the brake.

"I'll tell Bill Hammer all about it," he called down. "And I'll see you back in Mineral come sundown."

The stage went away with a rush, the chilled horses eager in their collars. Art Wilcoxon said, "What now, Cleve?"

"Wait for stronger daylight and then take a look around."

They built up smokes and went quiet with their thoughts. There was nothing to guess about in this affair. The bait had been large and the holdups had hit with ruthless efficiency. There was no doubt in Cleve Fraser's mind that the holdups had intended to leave two dead men behind them, and thought they had, what with the first shot knocking Hoot McCall down the way it had.

"How many do you think knew the amount Styles had with him, Cleve?" asked Wilcoxon abruptly.

"More than were present at the sale. It was hours after the sale before the stage pulled out of town. Plenty of time for the word to travel. That trail won't get us anywhere, Art."

"Be a smooth trick for Mallory to get Bunch Grass Basin and then get his money back too," Wilcoxon growled.

"A conclusion too easy to jump at, Art. Safer to keep an open mind."

Wilcoxon spun his cigarette butt into the road. "You're dead right, of course. But a man wonders."

Day quickened its advance across the shivering miles. In the east a ragged spread of thin clouds began to reflect a faint flush of color. North, the distant Sentinels were a solid black anchor at the rim of things. In the sage near by a desert wren struck up a brief chatter of sound, then went abruptly silent, as though frightened at its own temerity. Far off a coyote mourned hungrily. The earth and its various markings took on a distinctness.

Afoot, Fraser began a careful prowl. Sign was fairly clear, and he was able to reconstruct things with reasonable accuracy.

"Three of them," he told Wilcoxon. "One blocked the road and shot Hoot McCall. The other two came up on either side of the stage and took care of Styles and the money. We'll see which way they rode after the job was done."

The trail led directly east, and Fraser and Wilcoxon followed at a jog through the rank but scattered sage.

"This," observed Art Wilcoxon, "ain't going to do us any good. You know where they're headed, Cleve?"

"Sure. Baker's Lake. This thing shows too shrewd figuring to have been cooked up on the spur of the moment. Maybe like it was planned weeks before the sale."

In the long view the desert seemed flat, but at close hand this was not so. It ran in long rolls, and there were crests and depressions which asserted themselves almost imperceptibly. Some four miles from the scene of the holdup Fraser and Wilcoxon topped one of these crests and the sun, just surging into view, struck a solid, reflected blaze into their eyes. Out ahead lay the sprawling extent of Baker's Lake.

At this time of year it was an expanse of water, at no place more than a couple of feet deep. A mounted man could ride across any part of it and never wet his boots. By midsummer, however, it would be only a mile-wide expanse of bleached and alkali scabbed hardpan. The horse sign Fraser and Wilcoxon were following led straight to the water's edge and into it. Fraser reined up.

"They went in together, Art, but they wouldn't come out that way. They'd scatter and come out at widely separated spots. With all this cattle sign around we'd never locate those spots. The trail ends here."

Wilcoxon nodded. "When Sheriff Bill Hammer shows up and wants to know, we'll tell him how far we came. This cattle sign—maybe we better take a little look around."

"No better time," agreed Fraser. "Come on!"

They worked south, then east around the ragged outline of water, which thrust a hundred different fingers into the sage. Out of any of these the bandits might have ridden, their sign mixed and lost in the cattle trails which cut back and forth. These trails puzzled Fraser somewhat, for as yet no single critter was to be seen.

With the bulk of the lake to the north of them, he and Wilcoxon topped the containing crest to the east of the lake and then saw plenty of cattle milling about across a long-running sage flat. Now also something whimpered through the air overhead, and in the distance a rifle crashed flatly.

Surprise held for a moment. Then the distant rifle belted the echoes around again, and this time the bullet spurted dust almost under the hoofs of Wilcoxon's horse. The animal whirled of its own accord and plunged back across the crest. Fraser spurred after it. Wilcoxon began cursing bitterly.

"Will I never learn!" he raged. "I could have strapped a rifle to my saddle before leaving home yesterday. Now here we are with just a belt gun apiece, while that so-and-so out there's got the range on us! Cleve, what have we ridden into?"

Fraser did not answer. He was already out of his saddle, moving over to an outcrop of rock on the ridge crest. He clawed his way up the gray spine of this and looked over. Immediately that distant rifle clamored again, and the bullet smashed solidly into the rock, the heat of its abruptly expended energy sending up a thinly acrid odor. Fraser dropped back and returned to his horse. "Let's circle," he said, grimly brief.

They put their horses to a full run and when some distance south cut over the crest once more. No more shots came, and they saw, far out, two bobbing riders racing east. The distance was long, a good six or seven hundred yards now, and this, combined with the fact that the sun still blazed in their eyes, made any identification hopeless.

Equally useless was the thought of pursuit. Even if he and Wilcoxon succeeded in closing the gap somewhat, Fraser knew that that rifle would go to work again, pecking away at them while they, with only belt guns, would be helpless in hitting back. So he pulled up again.

"It's going to be that kind of a year, Art," he said harshly. "We'll need a rifle under our leg at all times."

"Anyhow," said Wilcoxon, "they lost their nerve and rode for it. Let's take a look at these cattle."

They rode back up the flat, the cattle breaking out ahead and on either side of them. Fraser read his own brand and that of Alec Cormack's. Wilcoxon's Running W showed, as did Dab Shurtleff's Split Circle. A shaggy steer, charging across in front of them, carried Grat Mallory's Rafter X.

"Quite a gather," observed Wilcoxon dryly. "Just about everybody represented. On purpose or by accident would you say, Cleve?"

Fraser shrugged. "Could be the cattle bunched on their own. There's some grass showing in this flat. Yet somebody was interested who didn't want to be recognized."

"Think those two could have been mixed in with the stage affair?" Wilcoxon hazarded. "And maybe watching their back trail?"

Fraser shook his head. "Don't think so. The stage

holdups would have too much on their minds to be sniffing around a little bunch of cattle strays. And no point in watching back on a trail already gone cold. Probably we showed up just in time to keep a couple of wavering cowhands honest."

Riding back to town, Wilcoxon said, "We'll be smart to call roundup a little early, Cleve. Busy boys with hungry ropes won't be quite so ambitious if they know roundup crews are ramming here and yonder across the country. Give 'em a funny feeling in their necks."

"We'll have to buck a late storm or two," Fraser decided. "But I can stand the misery of a few wet roundup camps if it means protecting my own. We'll put the idea to Cormack and the others."

At Mineral they found the town restless and buzzing over the news of the holdup. Burt Statler called Fraser into his office for what new word he carried. Fraser told him all he knew.

"Jack Styles," said Statler soberly, "was a damn good man. They must have shot him down like a dog."

"Three times—in the back." Fraser nodded. "A dirty business, Burt."

The Cormacks, Fraser found, had left for home fairly early that morning, so he went over to Henry Poe's store and picked up his sack of grub. Poe told him that Hoot McCall was coming along and observed that Hoot was a lucky man.

Fraser said, "Country is roughing up, Henry."

When he had climbed to the elevation of Bunch Grass, Fraser rode a trifle warily, wondering if Grat Mallory had already taken steps to fulfill his threat of closing the

58

trail. But he saw no sign of riders anywhere, and the wheel marks of Alec Cormack's buckboard cut straight through.

Bunch Grass lay empty to the farthermost reach of the eye. There was a somewhat bare and desolate look to it now, but this would quickly change once the spring sun had a chance to work on it. Then grass knee high to a tall horse would lay in shimmering waves across it, and it would all be Grat Mallory's grass. Come summer, the green would turn to a golden tawniness, and the richness of its color would be the omen of its worth. It was the kind of grass cattlemen had warred over since the first range boundaries had been argued.

Thinking these things, Cleve Fraser could once more appreciate the canny wisdom grim old Duncan Fraser, his father, had shown, even from the first, in never wanting any part of Bunch Grass.

"It is better, my son," Duncan Fraser had once said to Cleve, "to have less, when that less is all yours, and so placed that other men will not likely covet it, than to claim to something that is very rich and which all men will want and try to take from you. I see more than grass in Bunch Grass Basin. I see black hatreds and bloodshed. That day will surely come."

The gaunt old Scotsman had not lived to see his predictions come true, but that day, mused Cleve Fraser, could easily be in the near offing. The trouble would not come over the question of ownership, for that issue was now settled. Grat Mallory and his combine owned it. Trouble, if it came, would be over what Mallory might now cast his eye on and, seeing it as something he wanted, begin to force an issue. For, as Soddy Joens had said, grass hunger was like gold hunger with some men. They could never get enough of it.

At Shield and Cross headquarters Alec Cormack and his foreman, Sam Tepner, were checking over some necessary repairs of feed sheds and corrals caused by the past winter's ravages. Cormack asked for the latest on the stage holdup. Fraser told what he knew and also told of the cattle he and Art Wilcoxon had run into out by Baker's Lake and of the long-range rifle fire he and Wilcoxon had met with.

"Barefaced as that, eh?" growled Cormack. He brooded a moment. "Quicker we set honest riders to combing the range the better herd count we'll come up with. I'm ready to call roundup any time."

Passing the ranch house on his way through, Fraser saw no sign of Leslie Cormack. Never one to parade a hurt before others, yet there was a great capacity for depth of feeling in her. If she knew the need for tears, no one else would see them, for she had strong pride. Vance Ogden, mused Fraser a little savagely, should have stayed on for that supper in town.

Of course he himself was to blame to some extent. He'd used the rawhide on Vance, who had gone off angry. So they were both responsible for laying the shadow across Leslie's stay in town. Damn the pair of them!

Well, that was life, it seemed. No trail was ever completely smooth. Everyone was bound to know a certain amount of hurt. Still and all, some of that pain wasn't necessary. He stirred restlessly in his saddle, again highly dissatisfied with himself.

It seemed to Fraser that the sun had grown a little less bright. He looked up and saw that a thin rime of haze was beginning to stain the sky. Winter was in full retreat all right, but it still had a few shots left in its locker. A push of air coming down off the Sentinels had an antagonistic feel to it. Before morning a cold rain would probably be falling. Fraser set the dun to a faster pace.

4. The Real Power

JERRY PINE BROUGHT THE STAGE BACK FROM BREED'S Junction through a cold dusk and braked to a stop before the Timberline Hotel. Sheriff Bill Hammer was the first passenger to climb down. He was a tall, deeply browned man, taciturn of expression, with deep-set and coldly blue eyes. He turned and held up his hand to aid a slim, warmly coated figure through the fairly lofty swoop to the ground. Then he touched his hat and went around to the luggage boot to claim his valise.

A third passenger left the stage, a man of medium height, in overcoat, muffler, and dark hat. As he took the girl's arm and moved up the hotel steps, he suddenly seemed a bigger man than his size warranted. It was in the way he carried his head and shoulders, in the ordered certainty of his every move. He paused at the hotel door to let his glance run back down the street and over the darkening outlines of the town. Then he went on in.

As gaunt Jonas Cain met the newcomer's glance across the register desk, the hotelkeeper knew a slight shock. Never had he looked into eyes as cold as these nor met a glance which carried such authoritative impact.

"Two rooms," said the newcomer. "Adjoining ones. For my niece and myself."

"Sure," said Jonas Cain. "Seven and nine. They're front and the best in the house."

Precise writing ran across the two lines of the register. Pardee Dane. And then below—Miss Sherry Dane.

"You'll bring our luggage in," said Pardee Dane.

It wasn't a question and it wasn't a request. It was a flat statement. And there was significance in the fact that Jonas Cain, who had lived in the belief that every man could carry his own luggage, nodded and said, "Sure. Sure, Mr. Dane."

As Pardee Dane and his niece left for their rooms, Sheriff Bill Hammer came in and spoke with his quiet drawl. "Evening, Jonas."

Jonas Cain tipped his head. "Been expecting you, Bill. Mean business going on."

"Yeah," agreed Hammer briefly. "Mean." He glanced at the register. "New one on me. Pardee Dane. Never heard the name before."

"Me neither." Cain's tone was grumpy. "Sure seemed to know exactly what he wanted. Number four suit you, Bill?"

The sheriff shrugged carelessly. "Anything that's got a bed in it will do." Then he nodded, almost irrelevantly. "That girl is a raving little beauty."

The hotelkeeper grunted. "Didn't pay much attention to her. That fellow Dane seemed to fill the whole damned room. Now I got to go haul in their luggage."

At eight o'clock that night Grat Mallory rode into town and went straight to the hotel. He still carried the strong marks of Cleve Fraser's flailing fists, and Jonas Cain eyed him across the hotel bar with no particular friendliness and considerable satisfaction.

"Fraser always was able to swing a tough fist," said Cain.

Mallory flushed darkly, eyes glinting. He'd taken a look at the register in passing, so was sure of his ground. "Some friends of mine have arrived in town, Cain. The Danes. I want to see them."

Jonas Cain shrugged. "Help yourself. They're your friends. For a cowpoke, you fly high. Your friends are damn critical. Remind them that this is cow country, will you? It's the alkali in the water, not age, that makes the sheets yellow. And no better table is set in the territory. If they don't like my hotel, they can leave."

Mallory went along the hall, and it was the girl who answered his knock. "Grat! How are you? Uncle Pardee is expecting—" She broke off, staring up at him. "Your face? What happened?"

Mallory looked down at her hungrily. "It's the same old face, Sherry. Been bumped around some, but that doesn't matter just now. Girl, you got no idea how good you look to me!"

He caught her by both arms, half-lifted her toward him, but did not go through with the motion when, in the room's far corner, Pardee Dane cleared his throat with some emphasis. The girl covered the moment with a light laugh. "Same old Grat. Rough and in a hurry."

She was small and graciously made. Her hair was

black and fine and held a soft, sleek sheen. Her features were delicate and almost too perfectly carved, and her eyes were deep and black against an ivory skin. They were eyes that held many things—things no man could clearly read.

Mallory dropped his hands. "It's been a damned lonesome trail, Sherry."

He moved past her across the room, hand outstretched. "You arrived right on time, Mr. Dane."

Pardee Dane's handshake was perfunctory, dry. He tipped his head. "Have a chair, Grat. Sherry, do you think you could while away an hour in the parlor of this thing they call a hotel?"

The girl caught up a scarf, whisked it about her shoulders. Half-laughing she said, "You're too critical, Uncle Pardee. I think it's quaint and quite fascinating." She threw Mallory another glance, then left, her small heels making a swift tapping as she went down the hall.

Pardee Dane closed the door and turned. "Well, Grat?"

"I got it, of course," answered Mallory. "Just as I told you I would. The others couldn't get together before it was all over."

Pardee Dane's eyes showed a glint of satisfaction. "Good! How high did you have to go?"

"Thirty-one thousand. And a bargain at fifty."

"Quite so." Pardee Dane carefully lit a slim perfecto. "How about the other prospects?"

"We'll have to let time develop some of them," said Mallory carefully. "Several are going to be pinched for range. They'll have to cut their herds or run up against the problem of overgrazing. And that won't make them any stronger. Cormack and Wilcoxon and Shurtleff will be the first to feel the effects."

"What's the general attitude?"

Mallory showed a thin smile. "Sore as scalded cats. We're going to be well hated."

Pardee Dane shrugged. "Used to that. Hate never won a war. Brains sit in the victor's chair. Who around here has the most of that type of weapon?"

"That's a tough one, Mr. Dane. None of them are exactly fools, not the ones who count. Let's say we caught them off balance. Now they could get together. If they do, we got a fight on our hands."

"All the more reason for us to push our advantage." Dane laid his frosty glance on Mallory. "By the look of your face you've already seen some battle."

Mallory flushed, and a glitter leaped into his eyes. "There will come another time with that fellow."

"Then he must have licked you," said Dane. "Who is he?"

"Fraser. Cleve Fraser. He got the jump on me."

"Was he in on the bidding for Bunch Grass?"

"Not directly. He did offer to back Cormack's hand for ten thousand. But by that time Cormack was already in over his head so he turned the offer down. It was a friendship deal with Fraser more than anything else, for he's the one cattleman of size hereabouts who never has had any need of Bunch Grass."

"Where does his range run?"

"He winters over in the big bend of Stony Creek. But his best bet is up in the high parks of the Sentinels— summer range. There is one particular chunk that is very good, so I hear. Called the Garden. The cattle he brings off there in the fall are mighty good beef."

"So he's smart," said Pardee Dane softly. "Smart, and a fighter. He sticks by his friends, which is that sort of man's great weakness. You know, Grat, this fellow Fraser may be the real answer to our problem. I've handled several deals of this sort, and I've found there is always one man in the opposition who makes the big difference. He's the tough one, the hard one to corner and bring to heel. He's the keystone in the arch. When he falls, the rest crumble."

"That may be," admitted Mallory. "At the same time, Wilcoxon and Shurtleff aren't exactly soft. Cormack, well, he's getting along and has a wife and daughter to think about. In the last ditch he could turn salty, but it's my guess he'll be cautious at first."

Pardee Dane's cold eyes squinted against the smoke of his perfecto, then he held the cigar away from him and tipped the ash off carefully. This man was as fastidious as a cat.

"I've got the picture fairly well in mind, but I'd like a few angles freshened up. Here." Dane produced a pad of paper and a pencil. "Try your hand at a map."

Mallory discarded a couple of attempts before coming up with something that satisfied him. "All right," he said finally. "Here is Bunch Grass. This is how Cormack's Shield and Cross runs along the western edge of it. Fraser's lower Saber range is here, west of Shield and Cross and in the bend of Stony Creek—so. His summer range works all through the Sentinels up here. Wilcoxon's Running W and Shurtleff's Split Circle both touch the east line of Bunch Grass like this, and our present headquarters is here, on the old Tanner holdings. Pete Jackson's Triangle P J and Jim Lear's Lazy L are way over here on the fringe of things, and so is Vance Ogden's Square Diamond. The last three are all small stuff and don't count. Whatever real trouble we'll have will come from the outfits close-in and, as you say, maybe from Fraser."

Pardee Dane studied the map for some time in silence before speaking.

"In Bunch Grass we control the heart of the lower range. But until we also control the high range, nothing is really secure. You understand, of course, that Rafter X doesn't intend being limited to Bunch Grass Basin alone. That isn't the way I work. And when we start the squeeze on these lower outfits there must be no place for them to retreat to. For if there is, then we won't be able to break them. Oh, I realize that the high parks of the Sentinels are summer range primarily and that winter conditions up there could be very rough indeed. However, tough and determined men could hang on there after a fashion and so be looking down our throats all the time. Which we can't afford."

Pardee Dane paused to touch a match to his perfecto. "It's like I first said, Grat. This fellow Fraser and his Saber holdings form the key to our whole problem. Once we control that summer range of his, along with Bunch Grass, the rest will take care of itself. So—we go after Fraser!"

Grat Mallory stirred with a slight restlessness. "How?"

"By whatever means necessary to get what we're after," answered Dane curtly. "Primarily by weight of cattle. Within the next two months there will be a good fifteen hundred to two thousand head of Rafter X cattle on Bunch Grass. If necessary, we'll bring in more. But we won't hold them all in the basin. We'll test out that summer range of Fraser's with about a thousand head of them. When we start driving into the Sentinels, let's see him stop us!"

Grat Mallory was pretty much of a realist. He knew his own size, what he wanted from life and how he proposed to get it. He knew no shred of shame over his own evaluation of himself, but he owned to a queer, almost perverted pride which made him resent any other man being shrewd enough to guess his weight. That Cleve Fraser had been that shrewd the first time they met, Mallory knew, and he had hated Fraser accordingly from that moment. Now that Fraser had heaped on more coals by giving him a solid beating, man to man, the hate had become a raw flame. Yet, because he was a realist, Mallory did not let his personal feelings blind him to the hard facts.

"Fraser," he said, "won't whip easy, Mr. Dane. You might crowd his range to the last inch with Rafter X cattle, but you'd still have the man himself to reckon with. He's the sort, with all the chips down, to go right back to fundamentals, which means he'd strap on a gun and come looking for a target. He's the kind that you whip only by killing him."

Pardee Dane smiled without mirth. He purred, rather than spoke. "If necessary, that can also be arranged. I look forward to meeting the man face to face. It should be interesting. So much for that." He looked around the plain hotel room with open distaste. "Sherry and I are used to far more gracious surroundings than these and I see no reason why we should deny ourselves. So we are building a new headquarters at the site of the old army post on Red Bank Creek. There are busy days ahead, Grat."

Mallory, feeling that the talk was ended, stood up to leave. Pardee Dane stopped him with a wave of his hand. "You've done a fine job, Grat, fully up to what you did for me in Ruby Valley and on the Bidwell Plains. We'll have one drink to what has been done and another on what is still to do."

For two days and nights a cold, slanting rain whipped the range. When this storm broke, roundup chuck wagons began to roll. Cleve Fraser and his crew worked the bottoms of Stony Creek first, branding, tallying, and starting little gathers of cattle on the drift toward their home ranges. All across the country other outfits were doing the same.

It was hard, driving toil under a sky that stayed gray and bitter for several days. Another rain came up during a night and left men cursing soggy blankets and camp cooks swearing over guttering and slothful fires. But when this rain tailed off the skies cleared, the sun moved in with full, lasting force, and tempers improved.

Finished with the Stony Creek flats, Fraser and his men made a fast swing down into the desert to clean up about Baker's Lake. Part of the distance they covered by the Mineral-Breed's junction road and along this they met up with several heavy freight wagons loaded with new lumber and various other building supplies. Soddy Joens questioned one of the teamsters, then spurred up and dropped in beside Fraser.

"Headin' for the old military station on Red Bank Crick," reported Soddy. "Must be that Mallory is goin' to build a new headquarters there. He ain't wastin' no time setting up the capital of his empire."

As the outfit was about to leave the road and cut across the desert to Baker's Lake, a lone rider came jogging, heading for Mineral. It was Sheriff Bill Hammer.

"How!" he said laconically. "Rushing the season a bit, ain't you, Cleve?"

They shook hands. "All signs point to some early birds on the wing, Bill," was Fraser's significant answer. "Sort of figured to beat them to the proverbial worm. How's crime?"

Hammer shrugged. "Puzzling. Been out to take another look at the scene of the holdup. Thought I might stumble across something I'd overlooked before. The rain had washed everything out. What did you and Wilcoxon find, Cleve?"

Fraser told him all he knew, which was little enough. "They had it all figured, Bill, whoever they were."

"Would seem so," Hammer agreed. "Met our latest citizen yet?"

Fraser shook his head. "Didn't know we had one. Good or bad, this one?"

Hammer smiled faintly. "Have to wait a bit for that answer. I should have said citizens. Pardee Dane and his

70

niece. Friends of Grat Mallory."

Fraser stirred in his saddle. "That's interesting."

"Wait'll you see the girl," said Hammer. "Knock your eye out. Dane's as cold and smooth as they come. And snooty. He's been giving Jonas Cain a bad time. Nothing about the hotel suits him and he lets Jonas know it. Lot of new lumber moving north."

"To Red Bank Creek." Fraser nodded. "Looks like a new headquarters for Rafter X. This Pardee Dane, could he be the checkbook behind Mallory, Bill?"

"He's got the look of money about him," Hammer admitted. "Well, I'll be getting along. And Cleve, should you come up with any of these early birds you speak of, no necktie parties. Let me do the wrist slapping."

Fraser smiled grimly. "Bill, there's times when a guy like you are a comfort. And other times when you're a damned nuisance. But I'll try and remember."

At Baker's Lake they found Art Wilcoxon and his crew already at work. The combined outfits had the country clean in a day and a half.

"Next stop, Cleve?" asked Wilcoxon.

"Bunch Grass. Those willow flats along Red Bank should turn up quite a few head."

"Now I'll go you there," Wilcoxon said. "Things are happening in Bunch Grass, so they tell me. It'll be interesting to have a look."

The way north, bringing them close to Mineral, Fraser and Wilcoxon sent their crews on ahead and turned into town. Fraser told Wilcoxon about Pardee Dane, and both were curious for a look at the man. At the hotel Jonas Cain shook a bony head.

71

"Ain't here, Cleve. Mallory called for him and the girl first thing this morning. Took 'em off somewhere in a buckboard. Be all right with me if he never brings 'em back. Oh, the girl's all right, I guess, except she's almost too damn good-lookin'. But that feller Dane!" Jonas shook his head again. "Never had a man get under my skin so. Orders me around like I was a damn flunky and nothing about the place suits him. Abbie's ready to give him a piece of her mind too. She set a table for him and the girl last night with the best gear she's got, and when she saw this Dane hombre wipin' his knife and fork careful with his napkin before startin' to eat, I thought she was going to have a fit. I tell you it ain't natural for a man to be so damn fussy. Sure be glad to get shut of him." The hotelkeeper sighed lugubriously.

Fraser chuckled. "Guess we've spoiled you around here, Jonas."

On their way out of town again Wilcoxon pulled in at the High Front. "Just remembered. Dobie Roon asked me to bring him a pint. Swears that running a roundup chuck wagon and sleeping on the ground give him the miseries. Damned thin excuse, if you ask me. But he's a good cook, and if a little liquor will keep the old coot happy, why not?"

They stepped down and went in. Pipe Orr was fussing with bar chores. Vance Ogden and young Danny Cope were playing an idle hand of cards at a poker table. Wilcoxon went up to the bar and Fraser stopped by the poker table. It held a bottle and glasses and Vance's face was flushed. He looked up, met Fraser's glance briefly, nodded, and turned back to his cards.

"Lucky dogs," murmured Fraser. "Gentlemen of leisure. How do you do it in a cold, cruel world dedicated to the proposition that all men shall live by the sweat of their brows?"

Danny Cope laughed. "Could be the point of view, Cleve. Some men want more out of life than others. Some beat themselves over the head with a club and wear themselves out piling up a few extra pesos. Then they die and—what the hell?"

"Danny," jeered Vance Ogden, his voice slightly thick, "you're not ambitious. A week's whiskers on your jaw, your jeans soaked with horse sweat. That's the mark of prosperity. Didn't you know that?"

Both words and tone jarred Danny Cope. He looked up, caught the hardening glint in Fraser's eyes, and stirred uncomfortably. He tried to pass this thing off lightly.

"Don't think you got the answer there, Vance. I've been pretty frowsty myself and full of horse sweat, and I ain't prosperous. But I get along, which is all that counts, I reckon."

Fraser stared down at Vance Ogden, wishing they were alone so he could have told Vance a few things. But that would have to wait. He contented himself with a purely commonplace remark. "Art and me just came in from Baker's Lake, Vance. We turned up about a dozen head of your stuff. We cut it out and started it moving toward home range. If you get down there right away you'll be able to pick it up before it begins to scatter again."

Vance Ogden nodded, not looking up. "Plenty of time."

Fraser dropped a hand on Danny Cope's shoulder. "That riding job is still there, Danny—if you want it."

Danny said, "Thanks, Cleve. I'm still thinking about it."

Stepping into his saddle, Art Wilcoxon said, "Thought Ogden would be out riding cattle the same as the rest of us. He's not packing his weight, Cleve."

Fraser twisted up a cigarette. "Vance has his own way of doing things," he said carefully. "He'll move out one of these days."

Wilcoxon grunted skeptically. "Maybe. After the rest of us have done all the dirty work."

They were passing Henry Poe's store when Pio Cardenas showed in the mouth of the alley next door and called. "Señor Cleve!"

Fraser said, "Go on, Art. I'll catch up." He reined over to the alley. "What is it, Pio?"

Pio was plainly troubled, and seemed hard put to find words. "I try and be a good father. My daughter means much to me and I would see her happy all her days. I wish she was not so fond of Señor Danny."

Fraser leaned forward in his saddle. "Why, my friend?"

Pio hunched his shoulders. "A man with a wife must settle down. He must work steadily. Is that not so?"

"That's right, Pio. Danny is a good boy. A mite harum-scarum just now, but he'll steady down."

Pio's glance grew very direct. "Do you really think so, amigo? Or do you just say that to make Pio feel better?"

Fraser drew deep on his cigarette. Pio was longheaded and didn't fool easy. Pio had more on his mind than he'd yet disclosed. "Let's have all of it, Pio."

Pio spoke with careful slowness. "To have ready money in his pockets at all times a man must work. When he does not work, but still has money—well—!"

"I'm still listening," said Fraser, slightly harsh. "Go on."

Pio gave his native shrug. "You yourself said it had been a hard winter which scattered cattle badly. You said there might be some who would throw a hungry loop, Señor Cleve."

Fraser flipped his cigarette butt aside with some emphasis. "Sure of anything, Pio—or just guessing?"

"I can't help but put two and two together, amigo," said Pio doggedly. "And I do not like the answer. I hope I am wrong, amigo, but a man cannot fool himself." Pio looked extremely miserable, his black eyes clouded with woe.

"I'm glad you told me this," said Fraser quietly. "A kid can be thoughtless and full of foolish hell just for the devil of it. But that doesn't necessarily mean there's a real crooked streak in him. He's just a pup, chewing up a boot out of sheer devilment. A cuff on the ear can make a big difference. We'll look into this, Pio."

5. Cattle Trails

RAIN WHICH HAD CUT THE FROST OUT OF THE GROUND and a few days of steady sunshine had done its work on Bunch Grass Basin. The broad miles of Bunch Grass were now a green delight to the eye and the fresh vigor of new grass sent up a moist and vital fragrance. Viewing it, Art Wilcoxon almost groaned.

"When a man's made a damn fool of himself he hates to be reminded of it, Cleve. But I'll never run my eye across this basin again without being reminded—plenty! To think what a little common sense could have done, and then to realize what pigheaded stupidity really did, well—it sure twists the knife. The finest chunk of range on God's green footstool and Cormack and Shurtleff and I let it get away from us. We'll pay through the nose for the rest of our lives."

The chuck wagons were well out ahead, the crews trailing with the small remuda of extra saddle broncs. Cleve Fraser, riding tall in his saddle, gave everything within reach a careful survey. The green run of willow and alder thickets along Red Bank Creek were lifting ahead. Here there were riders and cattle. Well out to the right a gray scatter of buildings marked the site of the old cavalry headquarters, and here was definite activity, men moving about, piles of raw lumber shining in the sunlight, while a couple of big freight outfits unloaded more of the same.

Several riders broke away from the cattle along the creek, bunched as though for a short conference, then came spurring out to meet the roundup crews, who had pulled to a halt. Fraser and Wilcoxon moved up to their men and out ahead, and waited.

It was Grat Mallory, flanked by the ever-present Chess Breshear and Loop Scarlett, backed by another half-dozen riders, who had come in from the creek. Mallory waved his men to a stop, lounged easily in his saddle. The small mockery of his smile touched his dark, smooth face.

"Going somewhere?"

Art Wilcoxon grunted. "Come down to earth, Mallory. You know damned well why we're here and where we're going."

Over where the freighters were unloading, a buckboard pulled into movement and came spinning briskly.

Mallory, still with his mocking smile, said, "Believe I outlined some rules concerning Bunch Grass a while back. You hombres forgot?"

"Other things happened that same day," came back Wilcoxon tartly. "You forgot?"

Dark blood flushed Mallory's face, but he still held to his mocking smile. "I said you had ten days to get your strays off Bunch Grass, but no more. Time limit is up."

Cleve Fraser pushed his horse a little farther ahead. "Some of our cattle are along that creek, Mallory. We're looking them over and giving them the handling they require. To hell with your time limit. We're moving in— now!"

"Hah!" called Soddy Joens. "Now that is what I call laying it on the line. We're with you, Cleve."

That approaching buckboard was coming fast. Loop Scarlett growled something to Mallory, who swung his head for a look. Watching, Fraser saw Mallory's lips tighten. Then Mallory shrugged and locked his thoughts away behind blank eyes while he waited.

The buckboard came to a stop between the two groups. Pardee Dane held the reins in gloved hands. Sherry Dane sat beside him, dark eyes curious and missing nothing.

"An argument of some sort, Grat?" asked Pardee Dane.

Mallory's hesitation was very slight. "Little question of range rights, Mr. Dane."

"Mister Dane!" murmured Art Wilcoxon. "Now we know where Mallory got all the cash he had in his little satchel the day of the sale, Cleve."

Pardee swung his glance to Fraser and Wilcoxon. "What is your purpose here?"

Fraser had been looking this man over carefully. Now he gave it back to him, bluntness for bluntness. "Going to comb the creek bottoms yonder for strays."

"On what authority?"

Fraser went directly harsh. "On the authority that a man's cattle are his own, wherever he finds them. Old-fashioned custom of the range, you might say."

"And you believe some of the cattle along the creek will be yours?"

Fraser's lip curled slightly. "Imagine I'll shake up a few carrying the Saber brand."

"Saber!" said Pardee Dane. "Then you must be Fraser?"

"Correct. Cleve Fraser. Meet another fairly reputable citizen—Art Wilcoxon. And who might you be?"

There was that in Fraser's tone and manner which brought just the slightest flush to Pardee Dane's face. Here, he realized, was a man with a pride which, while not so flamboyant as his own, was just as steely and unyielding. He studied Fraser carefully for a long moment.

"I am Pardee Dane," he said finally. "I hold considerable interest in this basin. Also the authority to say who shall or shall not ride across its acres."

"Now," drawled Art Wilcoxon caustically, "we've got two emperors. Big one and little one."

The flush in Dane's face deepened, and a flutter of bare anger touched the dry severity of his cheeks.

"You're a stranger," said Fraser crisply, "and therefore can't be blamed for not understanding the common courtesies of the range. Mallory should have explained such matters to you."

For the first time Fraser's glance left Pardee Dane, to rest on the girl sitting the buckboard with Dane. Her dark eyes met Fraser's scrutiny, challenged him. This, of course, was the girl Sheriff Bill Hammer had told him about. Hammer hadn't exaggerated her good looks any, thought Fraser. She certainly was a raving little beauty, and Fraser felt his pulses stir. Fraser smiled faintly, touched his hat. Then he twisted in his saddle, glanced back at the waiting crews, gave his left arm a forward wave.

Wagons and men started to move. Fraser rode straight at Grat Mallory, forcing Mallory to swing aside and give ground. Art Wilcoxon did the same with Chess Breshear, while Soddy Joens, coming up fast, gave identical treatment to Loop Scarlett, saying in his lugubrious way, "Don't clutter up the trail, man."

The men behind Mallory gave way silently and the roundup crews moved through. From the seat of the Running W chuck wagon cantankerous old Dobie Roon grinned derisively and shot a stream of tobacco juice that splashed on a front hoof of one of Pardee Dane's buckboard team.

Banked fury gave Grat Mallory's face a swollen, congested look. He glared after Fraser with eyes so blank as to seem almost unseeing. Pardee Dane had to speak twice before Mallory jerked around. Dane was sitting stiffly upright on the buckboard seat, his face graven. Sherry Dane's glance was following Fraser, and Mallory did not miss that, either.

"There will be no further interference with those men now," said Dane. "I'll see you at the hotel tonight, Grat."

Mallory's voice sounded thick. "Give me the word, Mr. Dane, and I'll call Fraser's damned bluff right now."

Dane shook his head, spoke sharply. "Come back to earth, Grat. The man's not bluffing. Starting gunplay now wouldn't solve a thing. I have other plans. The hotel—tonight!"

Sherry Dane's glance touched Grat Mallory, read the boiling venom in him, then went again to Cleve Fraser's departing back. And the almost perfect curve of her lips broke into the faintest of small musing smiles. Then Pardee Dane had shaken the reins and the buckboard scudded away, its wheels drawing narrow lines across the new grass.

The Saber and Running W crews went straight on in to Red Bank Creek and set up camp in a small meadow. It was too late in the day to start a new gather, so Fraser told the men to rest and check up on their gear, while he and Wilcoxon took a look around. They rode easily along the creek, flushing cattle from the willow thickets. Both of their brands were in evidence, as were those of Alec Cormack and Dab Shurtleff. But the majority of the cattle were Rafter X.

"Mallory was damned sure of getting Bunch Grass

right from the start," observed Wilcoxon disgustedly. "By the look of things he's had most of his stuff moved in here for some time."

Fraser did not answer. He had jerked high in his stirrups, staring at a two-year-old that had just barged from a thicket. He spurred in chase, shaking out his rope as he went. He footed the animal neatly, upset it. Wilcoxon moved in, had a look, and swore softly. "Square Diamond, vented to Rafter X—and recent. What the hell—?"

Fraser twisted up a cigarette. "I don't know the answer either, Art. But as long as Vance Ogden isn't here to find out about it, I'm going to. Let's see if there's any more."

Fraser went back to his saddle, slacked off the rope. The two-year-old kicked free of the loop, scrambled up, and went off at a thumping run. Within the next twenty minutes they routed out half a dozen more critters with the same original brand, now vented to Rafter X, and all of it prime young stuff.

"If Ogden's doing legitimate business with Mallory, he's sure selling off his best beef," said Wilcoxon.

Fraser pushed his horse out of the willows and set off at a lope for the old military headquarters, Wilcoxon speeding up behind him. A couple of freight outfits, finished with their unloading, were pulling out for town. Late afternoon's haze was beginning to smoke up the world. Grat Mallory was in his saddle, giving his men some last instructions about something. He swung his mount around to face Fraser and Wilcoxon. He'd mastered his rage and his face had become the old smooth dark mask. But his eyes were banked.

"If this is calculated as a friendly visit, Fraser, it's time wasted."

"Pure business, Mallory," said Fraser curtly. "Art and me stirred up a full half-dozen of Vance Ogden's stuff, vented to Rafter X. Seeing that Vance isn't here I'm taking it upon myself to ask—how come?"

"Ever see a vented brand before?" Mallory's tone held its twist of mockery.

Fraser struck a hard palm on the horn of his saddle. Harshness blazed in him. "Not interested in wisecracks, Mallory. I want to know."

"Not your business as I see it," retorted Mallory.

"I'm making it so. You got the right or you haven't. Which is it?"

Mallory stirred in his saddle, threw a glance over his waiting men. There was no telling what was working in his mind. A touch of the spurs sent Fraser's horse pushing right into Mallory's, making it shift a step or two. Here was the old pressure again. Art Wilcoxon swung deftly around to the other side, a slender man, very erect and capable under any extreme. Fraser hit hard with his words.

"Nothing will do but the truth, Mallory."

Grat Mallory studied the gray smoke in Fraser's eyes, then shrugged. "One of these days, Fraser, you're going to push that tough jaw of yours into something that'll surprise you. In the meantime, as long as you're so hot and bothered, take a look at this."

Mallory dug a folded paper from his pocket and handed it to Fraser, who read the wording on it swiftly. He read it a second time more slowly, then handed it back. He felt baffled, helpless. His only comment was, "See that you count straight, Mallory. See that you stop at fifty."

He swung his horse. "Come on, Art. Let's get out of here!"

As he rode away, Fraser's face was taut with anger and disgust. Over and over he muttered, "The fool! The damned, damned fool!"

Leslie Cormack rode down across the basin trail to town. A vigorous girl, she'd never been one content to sit around a ranch house. Things at Shield and Cross had been very quiet for days, what with her father and crew away on roundup. A single rider, Nate Lyons, had been left at headquarters to keep the necessary chores done up and an eye on things in general.

Viewing the restlessness that had been piling up in her daughter, Mother Cormack had shooed Leslie out. "Go into town and spend a couple of days with Abbie Cain. You're like something caged here. And Leslie"—here the older woman's voice grew wise and gentle—"I would tell you a few things you must expect of life. The first is patience. The second is that it's the nature of men to be thoughtless at times. Not that they mean to be, but the sheer problems of earning a living in this world are bound to take up much of their thinking. A woman must learn to understand that."

Leslie had not argued this point with her mother, for she understood all this. But out in the saddle alone, she told herself a trifle fiercely that there was a great deal of difference between thoughtlessness and utter neglect.

She hadn't seen Vance or heard a word from him since that day in town, the day she had ridden in with Cleve Fraser, the day of the sale of Bunch Grass, and the night of the little dinner party at the Timberline Hotel, which Vance had failed to attend.

Honest with herself at all times, Leslie catalogued the march of her feelings. At first disappointment and hurt. Then a smoldering anger, and now a bright shield of bitter pride. How much had a woman the right to demand of the man she was engaged to marry? Surely not more of his time than the realities of living legitimately allowed. Her mother was completely right in this. But certainly she had a right to more than days and days of unexplained and unreasonable neglect.

There was a queer, empty sense of forlornness in her as she thought of Vance Ogden, but there was also that barrier of pride lifting ever higher and higher. And this scared her, and she tried to hold it back and wring the strength from it. For she certainly did not want a quarrel to spring up between her and Vance!

Intent on her thoughts and with the miles sliding back steadily under the busy hoofs of her sorrel mount, Leslie was within a couple of miles of town when she met the Lockyear brothers, Trace and Nolly. They were heading up into Bunch Grass and the thin darkness of their faces jerked Leslie back to realities with a snap.

They were tall men, lank and high-shouldered, who always rode in surliness and behind a wall of reticence of their own choosing. They headquartered somewhere back in the Sentinels, traveled shadowy trails and lived, so Leslie had heard her father claim more than once, on the beef of better men. Their general reputation was as dark as their faces, though, so far, not enough had ever been solidly proven on them to put them out of circulation. And there had been a time once, on a former meeting, when Nolly, the younger of the two, had made himself offensive.

A little start of fear went through Leslie when she first saw them on the trail. Then her head came up and her eyes were straight ahead and proud as she reined aside to pass them. She felt Nolly's glance measuring her, but there was no word spoken and no attempt to block her way. Her heart was thumping and she drew a long breath of relief when she was well past them. She was berating herself for having known any fear at all when she understood why, perhaps, that the Lockyears had let her pass so easily. Coming up the trail at a jog was another rider.

Leslie had met Sheriff Bill Hammer once or twice. Now, as he swung off the trail and stopped, touching his hat, Leslie reined in and smiled at him.

"Sheriff Hammer! I'm glad to see you again."

Bill Hammer's eyes crinkled slightly. "Tough-looking pair riding up ahead. Now where would they be lining out for do you imagine, Miss Leslie?"

"Nobody knows where the Lockyears ride, or why," Leslie told him. "They aren't seen this low down on the range very often."

"So I understand," Hammer murmured. "Wonder what brought them out of the sticks?"

Leslie shook her head. "I'm glad you picked this trail today," she declared honestly.

"Hum!" mused Bill Hammer. "Now they wouldn't

forget their manners, would they?"

Leslie flushed slightly. "They did—once. At least one of them did. That was several years ago."

"Somebody speak to them about it?"

"Yes. Cleve Fraser did. Pretty emphatically too."

Hammer wagged his head. "Cleve would. I'll bet it was interesting?"

Leslie's eyes widened and darkened at the memory. "I was frightened half out of my wits. It was a terrible fight. Nolly Lockyear was the offender, and when Cleve went after him, Trace Lockyear jumped in to help his brother. Cleve whipped them both, dreadfully. They had to be carried away. But Cleve will always bear the mark of that fight. The scar on his face."

Bill Hammer wagged his head again. "A man would never mind a scar earned that way."

He would have gone on, but Leslie held him up with a question. "Any idea on who pulled that stage holdup, Sheriff? Or wouldn't you want to say?"

"If I had a single solid lead I'd be happy to yell it from the housetops," declared Hammer. "But not a thing yet, Miss Leslie. But the case will break. They always do. I'm just really getting down to work, you might say. Tell your folks howdy for me."

Riding on, Leslie thought that behind Bill Hammer's quiet face and cold blue eyes lay a bulldog tenacity that would never give up. It was comforting to know that a man like Bill Hammer carried the law in this country.

Town was quiet. Leslie left the sorrel at Jerry Pine's livery barn and went up to the hotel. Abbie Cain was sweeping the steps and she hailed Leslie with delight.

"Child, come here while I squeeze you. I'm so full of gossip I'm like to bust. And nobody understands a woman's need for talk like another woman. Men just don't know how to listen."

Leslie laughed. "I'll listen as long as you wish, Abbie. That's what I'm here for, to get all the latest news."

"She's pretty, honey," declared Abbie, giving the steps a final swipe with her broom. "Almost as pretty as you are. But there are depths to her I can't quite figure. I'm not altogether sure they are honest depths. Yet, maybe I shouldn't say that, for in some ways she's real nice. But that uncle of hers! I declare I never saw such a man. Fair gives me the creeps, he does, he's so gray and cold. And finicky! Land sakes! You'd think my hotel was no better than a stable. I and Jonas will certainly be glad when he's out of here."

"That's all very interesting, Abbie," teased Leslie. "But I haven't the slightest idea who you're talking about."

"You will," affirmed Abbie Cain, taking her by the arm. "Come inside and meet her. Miss Sherry Dane."

Sherry Dane was curled up in an armchair in the hotel parlor, reading. She looked up as Abbie Cain and Leslie Cormack came in.

Abbie said, "Miss Dane, I'd like you to meet Leslie Cormack. You two are near an age and should get along in fine shape."

Which went to show that while Abbie Cain possessed much homely wisdom, there was a limit to it. For beauty now looked at beauty, and there was an instant measuring of silken swords. It was beauty in strong contrast.

Sherry Dane, small and with almost a classical perfection about her. Meticulous in every detail of dress and manner. Contained of thought. Sleek.

And then this long-legged, vital daughter of the open range, clad in a divided skirt of khaki faded from many washings and a blouse of the same material, leaving the brown column of her throat open to the winds. Sunshine in her hair, in her cheeks, and the faultless clarity of far distances in her eyes.

Leslie spoke first and simply. "This is a pleasure."

"Of course," said Sherry Dane. "Please sit down and talk with me. Mrs. Cain has been very kind to me, but—"

"I know," said Abbie Cain, hastily and entirely without rancor. "But I'm just an old woman with lots of things to do."

And so the ice was broken, but those silken swords were still unsheathed.

Saber and Running W turned up plenty of cattle along Red Bank Creek which were not Rafter X. It took a couple of days of driving work before they were satisfied to move on. They had worked from west to east, and on this far border of Bunch Grass met up with Alec Cormack and his crew. Shield and Cross had worked out the upper end of Bunch Grass all along the timber fringes of the Sentinels. Tallies and experiences were exchanged, and Alec Cormack listened with interest to Cleve Fraser's account of the slight brush Saber and Running W had had with Grat Mallory when they first moved into the basin.

"You figure, then, that the money part of Mallory's cattle combine is this fellow Pardee Dane?" Cormack asked.

"Must be, Alec. He took the play right out of Mallory's hands."

"And Mallory," put in Art Wilcoxon dryly, "called him 'Mister.' No question, Alec. Dane is the real owner of Bunch Grass. Mallory is just a figurehead and has been all along."

"How did this fellow Dane measure up?" queried Cormack. "I mean, how did you figure him?"

"Nothing startling until you got a good look at his eyes," said Fraser. "Then he begins to get bigger. Cold as an iceberg, and maybe as powerful. We'll see as the weeks roll along."

Fraser considered telling Alec Cormack about the several head of Vance Ogden's cattle, vented to Rafter X, that they'd run across, and of the outcome of his questioning Mallory about it. Then, on second thought, he decided not to. No sense in getting the older man worked up. That was an angle Fraser would find out all about the next time he saw Vance.

The three outfits moved east, into the Chinquapin Roughs. Here, they knew, would be one of the main chores of the roundup, for the big drift of winter-driven cattle was always this way. Here was a wilderness of broken country, of tangled and cross-running ridges, which broke the fierce fury of winter gales and blocked the drift of snow. In the twisted gulches between the ridges was the chinquapin oak brush, shoulder high to a mounted man, which gave browse and shelter to the harried cattle. Around the southeastern fringe of the roughs ran the stage and freight road between Mineral and Canyon City.

At Grizzly Creek, near the edge of the roughs, they found Dab Shurtleff, Pete Jackson, and Jim Lear camped with their outfits. The combined crews would start the heavy chore in the morning. Around a central campfire that night someone mentioned the winterkill. Pete Jackson spoke up harshly.

"I never kick about winterkill. That's one of the hazards of this cow business a man has to take and get along with. What lumps in my craw is live cows packin' my brand that I've worked and raised that end up under the hungry loop of somebody else. God hates a damn cow thief, and so do I."

"On general principle, Pete, or have you been seeing things?" asked Fraser dryly.

"Both! I've seen things. So has Dab—so's Jim Lear."

"Such as—what?"

"Sign of a little bunch here, a little bunch there, driftin' away from the rest without any good reason," Jackson growled. "Hell, Cleve, cattle don't start scatterin' out of their own free will until later in the year when the grass begins to thin out. You know that."

Dab Shurtleff nodded. "Pete's right. I've seen what he has. Some people never learn, it seems. I never did like that kind of a chore, but if we don't stop it now it'll grow worse. Soon as roundup is over I'm looking into that thing plenty!"

"And me!" rapped Jackson.

Jim Lear, the firelight picking out the foxiness of his

thin face, nodded and spat. "A neck stretchin' or two can sure be a powerful convincer. It's an old remedy, but nobody's ever come up with a better one that I know of."

"Had a talk with Bill Hammer," offered Fraser briefly. "Bill suggests we go easy with that sort of thing. He may be right."

"Bill's just talkin'," Pete Jackson said. "Not his cows being stole. That's one angle of my business I aim to handle in my own way. Any man starts rustlin' knows the penalty if he's caught. So he can't kick when he gets it."

Jim Lear's laugh was thinly brutal. "They all kick when they're on the end of a rope, Pete."

Alec Cormack stirred restlessly, eying Jim Lear with open distaste. "Not sure I agree with the remedy," he said curtly. "Not at all sure. There must be other ways of handling such things."

"Name them," challenged Pete Jackson. "Alec, you've been at this cattle business a long time, long enough to know that some things never do change."

"Yes and no, Pete. Maybe I'm getting old. But that sort of thing is a pretty stern responsibility for any man to take upon himself. Too much chance for a mistake."

"Can't go along with you there, Alec," said Dab Shurtleff in his heavy, blunt way. "I'd never jump at conclusions. But if and when I catch a rustler with the goods on—he swings! I'll pull no punches or play no favorites."

"That," said Pete Jackson, "is the kind of talk I like to hear. How about you, Art?"

Wilcoxon shrugged. "We'll see."

Jackson swung his glance to Fraser. "And you, Cleve?"

Fraser frowned at the fire. The flickering light made his face all hard, bold angles and muted shadows. The driving work of the past couple of weeks had leaned him down, laid a leathery toughness all through him. He spoke slowly.

"I don't like to be rustled any better than the next man. I'm not sure what I'd do if the chips were down. But one thing I know. We're talking about rabbits when there's a bear in the brush. A little rustling won't ever break any of us, but there's something else loose on this range that might. Bunch Grass Basin and the men who are in it. They're an angle to really lose sleep over."

"Now," declared Art Wilcoxon, "we're listening to wisdom. I can see where I'm going to cut my herd or run up against the hard fact of overgrazing what range I got left. If that goes for me, it goes for most of the rest of you. And when any man has to start cutting down instead of building up, he sure as hell ain't getting any stronger or more prosperous."

"Which still don't mean I have to stand for bein' rustled," persisted Jim Lear. "And while we're unloading our chests, here's something else I don't like. Where in hell is Vance Ogden? He ain't turned in a lick of work that I know of on this roundup chore. I'm not going to bother my head about another of his damn critters that I run across. They can all drift to hell, far as I'm concerned."

Cleve Fraser swung his head. "All right, Lear. You leave 'em alone. My outfit will take care of Vance's cattle."

The whip snap in Fraser's tone was startling. Art Wilcoxon had a swift look at Fraser's face, then stretched and yawned. "Long day ahead. I'm turning in."

There were several long days ahead, cleaning up Chinquapin Roughs. Once the combined crews put the pressure on, the tangled country vomited cattle. Smoke of branding fires stained the sky from dawn to dark. Men grew sweat-stained, bearded, and silent, and the remuda broncs turned ribby and gaunt. Every other day the stage rolled along the Canyon City road, with Jerry Pine still filling in for Hoot McCall.

Mild catastrophe struck. Alec Cormack, trying to chouse a stubborn critter out of a particularly mean, brush-choked gulch, had his horse go down with him, and when they pulled Cormack clear his left leg was broken between knee and ankle. They did the best they could for him and carried him out to the stage road, flagging down Jerry Pine as he came through from Canyon City.

They got Cormack into the stage, made him as comfortable as possible, and then Fraser told Jerry Pine, "Hit the fewest number of chuckholes you can, Jerry, and deliver Alec to Doc Curtain *muy pronto!* Think you can stick it without help, Alec?"

"Hell, yes!" growled Cormack through taut lips. "Damned old fool that I am. After all these years in a saddle I had to go let a horse fall on me. Don't worry about me, Cleve. Sam Tepner will take over for Shield and Cross."

Jerry Pine, gathering up his reins, said, "Things happening at Breed's Junction, Cleve."

"Yeah—what?"

"Cattle being shipped in instead of out. White faces. Couple of big trainloads. I'd guess right on a thousand head. Grat Mallory's bossin' the unloading. Stay with me, Alec," he yelled down. "I'll make it as fast and easy as I can."

The stage rolled away.

Dab Shurtleff swore harshly. "All those cattle coming in on this range. What's it mean, Cleve?"

"It means the squeeze is on, Dab. The bear is coming out of the brush."

Shurtleff scowled. "The day of the Bunch Grass sale I said it shaped up that some of us could have lost our shirts. That hunch is still ridin' me."

6. *Fast Gun!*

THE CATTLE CAME BY WITHIN A QUARTER OF A MILE OF Mineral. Twelve hundred head of them, a long, ragged ribbon of red and white, crawling up out of the desert, facing the first upward lift of country that led to Bunch Grass. Riders at point, at flank, and in the drag.

Sitting her sorrel horse a couple of hundred yards back from the drive trail, Leslie Cormack watched the stocky animals plodding past and knew a queer hollowness of feeling. There was an ominous something about this somehow. A monster, writhing itself into the heart of this range. The first wave of a flood that could inundate everything.

Leslie had heard her father speak somberly of what the

loss of Bunch Grass could do to the fortunes of Shield and Cross, as well as to those of other established outfits near by. He had spoken of the probability of having to cut down the size of his own herd to keep it within the limits of the grass still available to him. But now here was this tide of new cattle pouring onto the range. Les was shrewd enough to understand the significance of it all. One outfit building up while others faced the stern necessity of cutting down. The signs weren't good.

Hoofs rattled up and stopped beside her. She turned her head and cried softly, "Cleve!"

He was just as he had come out of the Chinquapin Roughs. Shaggy, torn, toil-stained. Unshaven, gaunt, and grim. His face was expressionless as he watched. Leslie asked the same question of him that Dab Shurtleff had.

"What's it mean, Cleve?"

"It means that the old order of things that we've known so long is gone, Les. Beyond that—" He shrugged.

Through the space of time it took him to build and light a cigarette Fraser watched. Then he shrugged again and turned his glance to the girl. "How's your father?"

"Cranky as sin and full of cuss words because he'll have to stay put for a few weeks. Doc Curtain said the break wasn't too severe. He even let us take Dad home. Dad sent me to town to see what the news was. When I tell him about this"—she nodded toward the flow of cattle—"it won't make him feel any better."

Fraser asked another question. "Seen Vance lately?"

He saw her lips tighten slightly and a flutter of feeling cross her cheeks. "Yes," she answered, low bitterness in her tone. "He's in town. You'll probably find him in the High Front. He's there more than he's any place else."

"Les," said Fraser, "Vance has wandered a little on us. We've got to bring him back into the old tight trinity."

Her slim shoulders stiffened. "If he does come back, he must do so by his own efforts. I'm not dragging my pride around at my heels any longer."

"Pride is a fine thing, Les. But too much of it at the wrong time can cause more unhappiness—"

She whipped the glove off her left hand, looked down at the ring on her finger. "What does a ring like that mean?" she cried softly. "What bargain does a man make when he puts a ring on a woman's finger? Does he think it's like putting a brand on an animal—that it marks his complete possession and that from then on he needs pay little attention to what carries it? I've never been a demanding sort, Cleve, but if cards and liquor mean more than I do— I—I have my dreams, too, you know."

He tried to remember if he'd ever seen this girl cry. Now it was not openly, though a couple of tears did manage to squeeze by and trickle down her cheeks a bit before she could brush them away. He kept silence, dragging a little savagely at his cigarette. It was Leslie who broke the long pause.

"I'm sorry, Cleve. Are you heading home?"

"Later. Some things I want to do first. If you'll wait around I'll buy your dinner and then we can ride out later this afternoon."

She hesitated, finally nodded. "Very well."

The river of cattle was still snaking past, its voice a solid rumble, the breath of it raw and vital in the warm air. Fraser gave it a final glance, then turned back toward town, with Les Cormack beside him. By the time they reined in in front of Henry Poe's store, Les had pushed her feelings out of sight and seemed her old bright self once more.

As they ducked under the hitch rail, Sherry Dane came out of the store. She had bowed to the customs and dress of the country and done extremely well for herself at it. Her divided skirt was of tan corduroy with a silk blouse to match. Her black head was bare and sleek and in her hand she carried a white silk neckerchief, obviously newly purchased over Henry Poe's counter.

She laughed cheerfully at Leslie Cormack's startled glance. "I guess I look like I feel—all new and crinkly. But if I'm to live in this country, I may as well begin to look the part. I hope Mr. Cain will approve. He's been viewing me like I was some kind of strange foreign insect."

"You look stunning," assured Leslie. "Cleve, meet Sherry Dane."

"I've met Mr. Fraser before," said Sherry Dane. "Though not to talk to. You left Uncle Pardee in a fine fury that day on Red Bank Creek, Mr. Fraser." She laughed again.

Fraser grinned faintly. "As I remember, things were a trifle brusque. Hope you don't hold it against me."

"Not at all," she declared. "Uncle Pardee's arguments are his own. I never take sides in them."

Watching these two, this tall, hard-jawed man whom

she'd known so long and so well, towering above Sherry Dane, Leslie Cormack knew a faint stir of restlessness, for she was not blind to the faintly mocking challenge that lay in Sherry's dark eyes, nor to the fact that open appreciation of the girl's beauty showed in Fraser's glance.

It was a small, frightening moment for Leslie. Cleve—Cleve Fraser! He'd always been her champion, always there with a shoulder for her to lean on, always kind and understanding. What had she given him in return? Her friendship as a companion. But it was Vance's ring she was wearing. . . .

Leslie tried to shake herself back to realities. She had no real claim on Cleve Fraser. After all, life was life and men and women met and knew mutual attraction. But— and Les gulped slightly at this thought—she'd never seen Cleve look at any other woman but herself a second time. And now . . .

"Heads up, Cleve!" It was Burt Statler's voice, carrying high and urgent along the street.

Fraser came around with a smoothness which belied the speed of the move. He rolled up on his toes as though bracing himself, while his glance raked the street in swift searching. A lank figure lounged at the corner of the High Front. Trace Lockyear!

Another slid into view out of the alley next to Buckman's freight warehouse. Nolly Lockyear!

Both were armed, both were watching him. This, decided Fraser swiftly, could mean nothing or it could mean much. He spoke a trifle harshly, without turning his head.

"Les, get off the street! And take Miss Dane with you."

Les Cormack, knowing well the old feud which lay between Cleve Fraser and the Lockyears, paled slightly, while her heart began to thump.

"Come with us, Cleve," she said tautly. "Into the store. Then they wouldn't dare—"

"No use dodging it if they mean business," cut in Fraser. "They might try it later, when I wouldn't have both where I can see them. Get off the street, Les!"

She looked at him as he stood there, saddle whipped to a fine, steely edge, his face jutting beneath the slant of his hat-brim, dark with weather and whisker stubble, against which the scar on his cheek made rigid marking. The muscles of her throat seemed to twist and lock.

"Please, Les!" The words came out of Fraser almost roughly. "You tie my hands while you stay."

Sherry Dane, not fully comprehending, was staring, wide-eyed. She did not resist when Les took her by the arm and steered her back toward Henry Poe's door.

Fraser stepped out into the street and walked straight in on Nolly Lockyear. Burt Statler, wishing for a weapon he did not possess, swore helplessly. Then, because he was a man of courage who believed in his friends, he left his office door and hurried over toward the High Front. He sent his voice out ahead of him, throwing it at Trace Lockyear.

"I've got no gun, Lockyear. But damned if I stand by and see the pair of you gang Fraser. Don't make a break or I go at you with my bare hands!"

Trace Lockyear dropped his right hand on his gun,

made a sharp and cutting sweep with his left, as though he was brushing something aside. "Stay wide, Statler!" he droned. "Stay wide!"

Fraser, catching the move of Statler from the corner of his eyes, yelled harshly, "Burt, get out of there! Not your mix!"

Now it was Sheriff Bill Hammer who came out on the porch of the Timberline Hotel. In one cold-eyed glance he took in the significance of what was shaping up. He came down the street at a run. Trace Lockyear saw this and realized that things were getting badly off trail. The percentage now was all wrong. He lifted his shout in warning.

"Nolly! No play!"

Nolly Lockyear had been watching Cleve Fraser with a fixity which let him see nothing else. It could have been that he'd been waiting his brother's shout as a signal to start this thing, that it meant Trace was set and ready to rake Fraser from the side. Again, viewing Fraser's inexorable advance, perhaps the tension had built up in Nolly until it had become a force he could not hold back. At any rate, on the first word of his brother's shout Nolly went for his gun.

Fraser was in there with him, drawing in mid-stride and at Nolly's first flicker of movement. Fraser shot from a slight forward lean, driving a slug low. Nolly got off a shot, uselessly, for though he had made the first move, he was behind Fraser at the finish. A smashing force had whipped his right leg from under him, spinning him and letting him down heavily and all asprawl. Then Fraser was over him, kicking the gun from his hand before he could recover.

Sheriff Bill Hammer, still running, paused only long enough to catch Trace Lockyear by the shoulder and throw him hard against the wall of the High Front. With bleak authority, Bill Hammer grated, "Stay there!" Then he went loping on down to where Nolly lay, surly and helpless. Nolly was grabbing at his crippled leg.

Bill Hammer picked up Nolly's gun, looked at Fraser. "Either damned good shooting or pretty ordinary," he growled. "Accident or design?"

Fraser shrugged. "I knew I could get there first, so I held for what I got. I could see no percentage in killing him."

"Tender sentiments you may someday regret," said Bill Hammer dryly. But there was a gleam of approval in his eyes to belie his words. He turned and called to Trace Lockyear. "All right! You can come down here now."

Trace Lockyear threw a single shadowed glance at Cleve Fraser before bending over his brother. It was a glance no man could have read correctly, for Trace himself was not altogether sure of the feeling that lay behind it. One thing Trace was definitely sure of. Fraser could have killed Nolly and would have been justified in doing it. But he had not. He had shot a leg out from under Nolly and let it go at that.

Doc Curtain, old in the ways of men with guns and warned by the hard, throbbing rumble of the shots, was already picking up his satchel when Burt Statler stuck his head in at the office door. They came down the street together.

From the doorway of Henry Poe's store Leslie Cormack had missed nothing of the encounter, nor had Sherry Dane. Watching Cleve Fraser move in on that certain shoot out, something had come over Les Cormack. Out of nowhere it came, unbidden, an abrupt sense of understanding that crashed through all her senses like the strong, clear chime of a silver bell. It left her breathless, utterly still, her eyes growing big and dark with the stunned wonder of it.

Les saw other things. She saw some men come crowding out of the High Front. One of these was Vance Ogden. And though the other men came hurrying downstreet to form a curious circle around the fallen Nolly Lockyear, Vance turned abruptly and went back into the High Front again.

Sherry Dane gave a long, fluttering sigh. Her fingers gripped Leslie's arm, and she spoke in a small, tight voice. "Does—does that sort of thing take place often?"

"It probably will from now on," Les answered, coolly blunt.

"Why from now on?"

"Ask your uncle that—ask Grat Mallory."

Sherry Dane headed for the hotel, walking faster and faster, until she was almost running when she reached the Timberline. She dodged past Jonas Cain, standing in the doorway, and hurried to her room. From the window of this she looked along the street, now clearing. Men had carried Nolly Lockyear off somewhere. Cleve Fraser and Burt Statler were crossing to the latter's office. Sherry's eyes followed Fraser every step of the way, and when this tall, cold-jawed man, toil-toughened and rough, straight off roundup, moved out of sight, it seemed she could still see him.

She could still see him, grimly harsh, prowling across to meet Nolly Lockyear, and she knew it was a picture she would never forget in all the run of her life.

In his office Burt Statler dropped into his desk chair with a little sigh of relief and lifted a thin smile to Cleve Fraser. "Man! I'm glad that's over with. It'll take the rest of the day to get the shake out of my knees."

Fraser eyed him gravely. "Owe you one for that, my friend. Warning me and moving in on Trace Lockyear with empty hands took guts."

Statler waved a limp hand. "Think nothing of it. I was scared stiff—still am. What set those Lockyears off?"

Fraser built a smoke, face sober. He shrugged. "Never has been any love lost between them and me. Maybe they been thinking on something of the sort for a long time and just had to bust loose."

"I got to wonder about it," said Statler. "May be my legal training that makes me suspect motives. Anyhow, I'm mighty glad it ended up no more serious than it did." The lawyer settled deeper in his chair. "I've been wanting this chance to talk with you about this Pardee Dane, Cleve."

Fraser perched on a corner of the desk, swung a booted foot. "What about Pardee Dane?"

"I've been checking up on the man," explained Statler. "Curious cuss—that's me. I've written some letters, and I've found out a few things. The man is powerful. He's got money and some connections that reach clear to

Washington. I find that Bunch Grass isn't the first piece of government land he's bought up. There was a big chunk he acquired cheap in Ruby Valley up at the northern end of the state, and another over on the Bidwell Plains. He seems to get advance dope on the sales from Washington and is all set to grab these rich prizes before the little fellows can get organized."

"Shrewd operator." Fraser nodded briefly.

"Yeah," agreed Statler, "shrewd. The story goes deeper. The man seems to work a certain system on these deals. He gets the central chunk of government range, gets well dug in, and then starts putting the pressure on all the smaller outfits round about. One way or another he discourages them, and the first thing you know he's gobbled up the entire stretch of country. That is the way he has worked it in Ruby Valley and on the Bidwell Plains. With such a scheme working well in those places it's logical to expect some of the same sort of business here. So watch yourself, my friend."

Fraser took a final deep inhale of his cigarette, then crushed out the stub in an ash tray. "Why warn me, Burt? I'm way out at the edge of things. No range of mine comes within miles of Bunch Grass. If Dane has got ideas bigger than can be held inside the limits of Bunch Grass, the men he'll be looking at are Alec Cormack, Art Wilcoxon, and Dab Shurtleff."

"Probably he is looking at them," said Statler, "and while none of them are what you'd call gentle kittens when the chips are down, the real tough man on this range is you, my friend. Oh, don't let your modesty try to argue with me, for I'm an unbiased observer and so able to see all men in their proper stature. And your shadow runs considerably longer than that of any of the others. You're the one who could be the core of opposition, and if I can see that, let's give Pardee Dane credit enough to be able to figure out the same answer."

Fraser smiled grimly. "I think you're full of bug juice, but for the sake of argument, if what you say is so, what would Dane do after he'd figured such an answer?"

"If he's as smart as I think he is," answered Statler bluntly, "he'll realize that you're the first one to put out of business. You'll be smart to govern yourself accordingly, to keep an eye on the man, and translate every move he makes in terms of how that move could affect you."

Fraser slid off the desk, prowled to the door, looked along the street. There was no more dust lifting over where the newly arrived herd of white-faced cattle had passed. But from the lift of country above town, faint with distance, the voice of that herd came back as a faint echo. Into Bunch Grass the herd was going. But was that to be its final destination? Would it stop there?

Fraser turned back, scrubbing a hand along his whiskered jaw. "So you've given me something to worry about," he growled. "We'll see. But now I've a question for you. Burt, what are we going to do about Vance Ogden? He's your friend and my friend, and somehow he seems to have got off the trail on us. We got to haze him back on to it."

Statler looked at Fraser steadily. "Glad you brought that up, Cleve, because I didn't want to. Now that you have, I'll say this. Vance has never been to me what he has to you, so I'll make no excuses for him. Flatly, he's been making a damn fool of himself. All winter he's hung around town, gambling like a crazy man. He's lost his shirt. Stack Portland has called his notes, closed him out."

Fraser's tone went quickly savage. "The devil you say! Then I see Stack Portland as a damn—!"

"No," cut in Statler. "You're wrong, Cleve. Stack Portland is a square, lenient, and just man. He's been more than lenient with Vance Ogden. He's carried Vance far beyond what good banking practice calls for. Put the blame exactly where it belongs, which is on Vance alone. Your long friendship for Vance inclines you to overlook a lot. Other people see him for his true worth, or lack of it, more clearly than you do."

"Granted I'm prejudiced," rapped Fraser. "Just the same, because a man's begun to slip a little is no reason—"

Statler cut in again in that same quiet, steady way. "I'm saying this for your own good, Cleve. A man can break his own heart trying to hold up a friend who hasn't the backbone to do the job himself."

"Still and all," said Fraser harshly, "he's a friend. And to me that means something. Thanks for everything, Burt. Be seeing you."

He went out, his stride purposeful, and headed directly to Stack Portland's bank. Stack saw what was in Fraser's face and held up an admonishing hand.

"Don't say it, Cleve. It wouldn't do any good. There's a limit to any man's patience, and mine has long since run out with Vance Ogden. I've warned him half-a-dozen times to spend his time working his ranch instead of in the High Front playing poker and lapping up booze. I've loaned him money in good faith. He's kicked that faith into the gutter. I'm done with him!"

"How much does his notes amount to?" asked Fraser bluntly. "I'll buy them from you."

"No, you won't," said the banker. "That's for your own protection. It's all settled, Cleve. I'm sending a good man out to the Square Diamond to take over for me."

Stack Portland had a head of snowy hair, with level eyes set in a square-hewn face. This man was kindly and he was fair. But he was no fool. And once he'd made up his mind to what he thought was just and right, there was no swaying him. But there was another angle, and Fraser spoke of it.

"You've been here a long time, Stack. You've seen this range grow up and you know the people of it well. In this deal about Vance, maybe he's not the only one I'm thinking about."

"I know that, Cleve, and it's the same way with me. She deserves better than Vance Ogden, and perhaps this is the best way of making her realize it. I'm thoroughly honest in this."

Fraser stared into nothing for a long time, then murmured, "I know that, Stack. Sorry."

Stack Portland dropped a hand on Fraser's arm. "It made me feel mighty good a little while ago, boy, to see you standing fine and untouched after the smoke had cleared. I hope it will always be that way with you."

From the bank Fraser went over to the High Front. A

few men were there and the talk was all of his shoot out with Nolly Lockyear. They quieted, though, when Fraser came in and walked to a far corner where Vance Ogden sat alone at a poker table, idly setting up a game of solitaire. Fraser took a chair across from Vance, leaned forward with his elbows spread on the table top.

"We're going to have a straight-from-the-shoulder talk, fellah. In here or out behind the woodshed—which will it be? But we have that talk!"

Vance lifted his head, looked at Fraser, then his glance slid away. "Here is good enough for me. But for God's sake don't try to preach. I won't stand for that."

There was roughness in Vance's tone, and a thin hostility. Fraser studied him quietly. That handsome face was changing. There was the bloat and flush of too much whisky, for one thing. There were pulled, sullen lines about the mouth.

"A bargain." Fraser nodded. "No preaching, but no punches pulled, either. I understand that Stack Portland has called your notes, which you can't meet, and so is taking over your ranch. How about that?"

Vance shrugged. "Quite true. And suits me. Don't have to worry about the damned ranch any more. Anything else?"

"Yes. When working through Bunch Grass on roundup we ran across several Square Diamond critters vented to Rafter X. I called Mallory on that, and he showed me a bill of sale you'd drawn up. Damnedest thing I ever saw in my life. It allowed him to vent out fifty head of your stock. And you can bet he was picking the best of them."

"Why not? He'd be a fool to pick the poor ones. If the deal suits him and suits me, why should you worry?"

"Several angles to a thing like that," said Fraser. "First, what's to keep Mallory from going way over fifty head, as long as he's packing that stupid authorization of yours? But the bigger questions go further than that. What did you get out of the deal—cash money? Or was it to settle a poker debt?"

Vance did not speak, but he stirred slightly, so Fraser knew the answer. Bitterness roughed up his voice. "You pulled a stunt like that to pay a gambling debt! I'll bet Mallory suggested it, so he could rob you blind. Man, you need a keeper!"

Vance's head came up. "Don't you try to make yourself one. I'll get along."

Looking at this man and thinking back to so many good days in the past, Fraser felt some of the toughness run out of him. He leaned across and dropped a hand on Vance's arm. "Kid, let's quit snapping at each other. This thing can still be straightened out. Let's get together and clear the air."

Vance didn't soften a bit. Instead, he drew farther away. "If people would only mind their own damn business! Have I ever tried to tell you how to run your affairs? No! So get it through your head I want to be let alone. Any deal that comes between Grat Mallory and me is our own affair, nobody else's. Let it stay that way!"

Fraser leaned back, built a smoke. His face went stony. "All right. That's settled—for good. But I want an answer to one more question. When you made that fool bill of sale, had Stack Portland already called your notes?"

"I was waiting for you to get to that," said Vance harshly. "Yes—he had. To hell with Stack Portland!"

Fraser spoke almost softly, like a man merely arranging his thoughts. "The minute Stack called the notes and you couldn't meet them, ownership of every head of Square Diamond stock was transferred from you to Stack. You had no legal or moral right to sell them to Mallory under any kind of a deal."

"But I did it," mocked Vance Ogden. "So—what?"

"So you're crooked," gritted Fraser. "A damned thief. Stack was right. You kicked his faith in you into the gutter. You've kicked that of other people into the same place. If I thought it would do any good I'd drag you out of here by the scruff of the neck and whale hell out of you."

"Which you could probably do all right," agreed Vance, still mocking. "But it wouldn't answer anything." He shuffled the cards and began another layout.

Cleve Fraser had the feeling of punching at empty air. This man across the table from him wasn't Vance Ogden, not the old Vance he'd known. This man was a stranger, a slippery shadow you couldn't get hold of and nail down, no matter what kind of approach you tried. You reached for him and he wasn't there.

Fraser said not another word. He got up and walked out. Vance looked up and watched him go, marking the ruggedness of his head and shoulders. A shadow of regret formed in Vance's eyes.

"So long, old boy," he murmured to himself. "Rough

on you, but I don't know of any other way to make it final. My bed and I'll lie on it. And there never was any sense in going only halfway to hell. I can see now that the slide was greased from the very first. Because I never did have what it takes, and I haven't got it now."

7. The Bitter Tide

AROUND MIDAFTERNOON YOUNG DANNY COPE SAUNtered into the High Front, bought himself a beer and a couple of sacks of smoking, dawdled over his drink while talking a good deal of nothing with Pipe Orr. From time to time Danny swung his glance toward Vance Ogden, who still sat at his solitaire game. Finally he caught Ogden's eye and gave an almost imperceptible nod, then paid Ogden no more attention.

Some fifteen minutes later Danny rolled a smoke and went out, sauntering, moving with the fluid ease of young, supple muscles and with a reckless mind contemplating what lay ahead with a rising thread of excitement. He left town at a jog, heading east along the Canyon City road.

Half an hour later Vance Ogden left his cards, paused at the bar for a final drink. Pipe Orr said, "Should be a game tonight."

Vance shrugged. "Not interested the way these town sports play poker. A dollar bet scares them to death. They should stick to checkers."

Vance went out and was heading for his horse when Henry Poe came angling across the street. When he wanted to, the storekeeper could be blunt. He was blunt now. "I hear Stack Portland called your notes, Ogden?"

Vance hooked a stirrup on the saddle horn, set up a trifle on the latigo. "Seems to be common knowledge. What about it?"

"Three hundred dollars," said Henry Poe. "When I loaned it to you, you said a few days. How many is a few?"

To himself Vance said, "That's right. I'm down. Kick me in the teeth, damn you!" Aloud and shrugging, "Keep your shirt on. You'll have your money inside another week."

Vance stepped into the saddle, urged his horse to movement. Henry Poe stared after him, then turned and went back to his store, mentally writing off three hundred dollars.

Some three miles out of town the Canyon City road crossed a shallow wash in which the water had already ceased to run. The wash angled a twisting way to the northeast, and as it went along grew high banked enough to hide a mounted man. Half a mile along this Vance found Danny Cope waiting for him.

"Broke again?" demanded Vance grumpily.

"No," answered Danny. "But with the roundup crews heading back to their home layouts to rest up it looks like as good a time as any."

Vance considered, then nodded. "That's right. Where away?"

"Ought to be something stirring around the west edge of the Chinquapin Roughs."

"Let's go!"

They stuck to the wash for several miles then broke

out of it to the east and came down to Grizzly Creek. Here they began meeting up with cattle. They worked fast, cutting out good ones. By sundown they had thirty head in front of them, driving deep into the first timber coverts along the lower flank of the Sentinels. By the time the first stars winked through, they had the cattle bedded in a small, lonely clearing.

They watched the night out and were on the move again in the first of dawn's gray light, pushing the cattle ever higher and deeper into the mountains. By sunup the cattle were grazing in a fairly high meadow and Danny Cope stayed to guard them while Vance Ogden sent his horse climbing to a little benchland where the big timber thinned somewhat and a bank of quaking aspen spread its brighter green. Backed up against the aspens was a cabin and a pole corral. Smoke winnowed thinly from the cabin chimney and several horses crowded together in one corner of the corral.

Vance Ogden sent a call ahead and Trace Lockyear showed in the cabin door, a rifle across his arm. He put the rifle down and waved an arm. Vance rode in.

There were four in the cabin besides Trace Lockyear. One of these was Nolly Lockyear, blanketed on a bunk, his face drawn and peaked looking. Of the other three, one was a short-necked, bull-shouldered man with long arms and bowed, thick legs on which he moved with a sort of rolling gait.

"High time, Ogden," he growled. "Me and Frank and Hardy were getting tired laying around. Thought we might go out and look for some ourselves. How many this trip?"

"Thirty head. Cope's holding them down in the meadow."

"What brands?"

"Running W, Split Circle, Triangle PJ, and Lazy L. Saber and Shield and Cross stuff has all been pushed too far west to get at them without running the long chance."

One of the others said, "Hell with the brands. Beef's beef. We'll look at Saber stuff later on when Fraser and Mallory get to scrambling each other over the high range."

Vance Ogden looked at the speaker. "You think that will come, Hardy?"

"Come? Of course it will. Can't miss. Grat Mallory ain't the sort to stop short of whole hog. I hope it's a good tangle. We'll get our share, eh, Beede?"

Beede Helser's heavy jaw pushed out as he grinned. "We won't be picking posies. All sorts of deals to be made. Well, get outside that grub. Work to do."

Trace Lockyear poured coffee, spread hot food on plates. Beede Helser, Frank, and Hardy ate and drank, then went out to the corral, and soon the thump of hoofs vanished down the trail. Vance Ogden poured a cup of coffee, sipped it, and looked down at Nolly Lockyear.

"Tough on you, Nolly—having to come clear up here with that bad leg."

Nolly stirred slightly. "I'd have ridden to hell with it rather than stay in that damned town. Cain wouldn't let them put me in his hotel and I wasn't going to lay out like a dog in Pine's hayloft."

"I can't feel too sorry for you," Vance told him bluntly. "I warned you to let well enough alone with Fraser. Hate

114

him if you want, but you got to admit he's poison in a fight."

"There'll come another time," vowed Nolly.

"No," differed Trace Lockyear. "No, there won't. He could have killed you, Nolly—and he didn't. He just shot a leg out from under you. I ain't never going to walk up to Fraser and kiss him, but I'm remembering that he could have killed you and he didn't. So, from now on Mallory and that boss of his, Pardee Dane, can hire somebody else to carry the torch against Fraser. You and me, we're out of it."

Nolly closed his eyes and said nothing more.

By the time Trace Lockyear had more food cooked up, Danny Cope rode in. He dropped a bundle of rumpled currency on the table. "Helser said we did a good job of picking them, Vance."

Trace Lockyear divided the currency into three piles, counting as he went. He pocketed one of the piles, Danny and Vance taking the others. "Nice night's profit," said Trace briefly.

They ate in silent, hungry absorption. Finished, Danny Cope built a cigarette. "I told Helser not to get too impatient for the next drag. We've been pushing our luck a little. Be smart to let things quiet down a little. Besides, we got to remember that Bill Hammer is prowling constantly and he's nobody's fool."

Nolly Lockyear opened his eyes and rolled his head. "Hammer ain't worrying about cattle tracks. He's after bigger game."

"That's right," conceded Danny. "But the man's got good eyes and plenty of savvy, and he bobs up at the damnedest times and places."

"I wonder if he's learned anything about that holdup?" Vance Ogden murmured.

"I wonder if anybody has?" said Trace Lockyear.

"If you had one guess, who would you tag as having pulled it, Trace?" asked Danny Cope.

Trace brooded a moment, then shook his head. "You got me there. If I had twenty guesses I doubt I'd even come close."

Lying back in Frenchy Payette's barber chair, Cleve Fraser let his eyes close under the comfort of Frenchy's deft, keen razor. Fraser was relaxed physically, but his thoughts kept running. He was recalling what Henry Poe had said one time about poker.

A little of it never hurt any man, but too much of it could tear him apart. Poe had been so right. A man's future, the respect of his friends and of those who counted, had gone to hell across the tables in the High Front. Vance Ogden's future. And what could he or anyone else do about it? And what about Leslie Cormack?

That was the angle that twisted the knife. As fine as his friendship with Vance Ogden had once been, Fraser was realist enough to know that he could push that part of it into the background and cover it with time and the future's always insistent activities. He would know regret, of course, but the world turned and life went on and a man's rugged code had a core tough enough to absorb jolts of this sort without permanently damaging effect.

But when a woman as fine as Les Cormack had staked her future and her brave dreams on a man who was turning out to be the weakest sort of stuff, then what? How deep would the wound be there, and how long lasting?

Fraser stirred and through the lather said, "Frenchy, it can be a stinking, lousy world."

Frenchy said, "You work too hard, Cleve. Take time out to laugh and look at the sky. Big country up there, clean and full of sunshine."

Finished with his shave, Fraser went up to the Timberline, his mood still somber. Abbie Cain met him at the door.

"Land sakes, Cleve Fraser, you can scare a body half to death. Did you have to walk across that street after that worthless Nolly Lockyear?"

"A man has to cross a street every once in a while, Mrs. Cain," answered Fraser briefly. "Les Cormack around?"

"No, Cleve," said Abbie Cain carefully. "Les has gone home. She told me to tell you and ask that you please excuse her for running out on your dinner invitation."

Fraser was still for a moment, then nodded. "She had her good reasons, I guess. That isn't like Les, though."

"No, it isn't," agreed Abbie Cain. "But be generous about it, boy. Les has been taking considerable of a whipping of late."

Meeting Abbie Cain's kindly eyes, Fraser nodded. "I know. And I'd never hold anything against Les."

He went on in to the dining room and saw Sherry Dane just pulling her chair up to a table. She looked at

Fraser and smiled gravely, holding his eyes while he paused beside the table.

"I wanted this chance to tell you, Mr. Fraser, how glad I am that it was you and not that—that other man who was able to walk away. I don't believe I was ever half as frightened before in all my life."

Fraser was startled. "Why, that's right nice of you, Miss Dane." Then he added, "Pretty rough thing for you to see."

She nodded soberly. "I'd heard that such things happened. But I always believed such stories exaggerated. I know better now. Is there any good reason why we should eat alone?"

Her dark head held the silken shine of a blackbird's wing. Her beauty was as real as sunshine. Fraser pulled out the chair opposite her. "Aside from your uncle I can't think of anyone who might object."

She laughed softly. "Uncle Pardee's control of my affairs is less than you think. We have a bargain that way. I don't interfere with his activities, nor he with mine."

Fraser sat down. "From the neck up I'm reasonably presentable. From the neck down I'm a tramp."

Her laugh held an amused lilt this time. "A strong man's strength needs no gloss. I prefer the reality of you. I'm going to enjoy my dinner, even if I am second choice. Oh yes—I know you expected to eat with Miss Cormack. I overheard her explaining matters to Mrs. Cain. I hope I'm an acceptable substitute."

Fraser showed her a small grin. "We'll get along, Miss Dane."

"Make that Sherry, please. I intend to call you Cleve.

I hate formality. I've had so much of it all my life. I find the ways of this country and its people very refreshing."

"Except," murmured Fraser, "when a man has to cross a street?"

She shivered slightly. "Yes, with that exception. Now, tell me about yourself, Cleve."

He shrugged. "Nothing much to tell. Just a four-bit cattleman. Got a few friends and some enemies. Ordinary as an old boot."

She surveyed him critically. "I could argue with you there. Ordinary people don't thrive in a country like this. For instance, Miss Cormack. She's wonderful—the most vital person I've ever known."

Fraser nodded. "There's only one Les Cormack."

"You've known her for a long time?"

"Considerable. We more or less grew up together. The world has been a good place to live in because of Les."

Sherry Dane caught her breath slightly. "You may not realize it, Cleve, but that is the nicest compliment I ever heard spoken for anyone."

They talked of many things, eating leisurely, and Fraser forgot momentarily that this girl was the niece of the man which all signs pointed to as shaping up as the core of an influence that bade fair to tear the range apart. No man could remain unmoved by the sheer beauty of her, by her quick, tinkling laugh, her agile mind. In short, Fraser enjoyed himself.

That he did was plain to the eyes of Abbie Cain, moving busily in and out, and to herself Abbie murmured, "Careful, boy. There can be claws under the velvet. I'll wager she's made more than one man dance

119

at the end of her string."

The meal done with, Fraser pushed back his chair. "It's been mighty pleasant, Sherry. Reclaimed a day that's had considerable gloom here and there."

Sherry gave her soft laugh. "Now I feel that Leslie Cormack hasn't all the good luck. For I've had my compliment too. A nice one. I'll see you again, Cleve?"

He grinned. "Unless I break a leg."

As he turned toward the door of the dining room, Fraser's grin wiped out, for Grat Mallory was standing there, dust- and sweat-stained from the cattle drive across the desert. His smooth, dark face was impassive, but it was plain from the hard glint in his eyes that he had not missed the fact that Cleve Fraser and Sherry Dane had dined together.

Fraser gave him stare for stare and moved past him, neither speaking. Mallory went along the room to Sherry's table, took the chair Fraser had just vacated.

"You've eaten, of course," he said, unable to keep all the roughness out of his voice. "I'd hoped for this pleasure myself, Sherry. And you gave it to Fraser."

Her answer was quick, coolly curt. "First, I don't like your tone, Grat. Second, I've never posed as a mind reader. How was I to know you'd be in town? Finally, what gives you to believe you have any right at all to say who I should or should not dine with?"

Mallory rubbed a hand across his face. "Didn't mean it that way, Sherry. But I've been working like the devil and hoping to have a little time with you now and then. Jolted me to see you with Fraser. He's the enemy, you know."

"To you and Uncle Pardee, perhaps," she replied tersely. "But not to me. He's a big man, Grat—and he walks with long strides. I like that sort of man."

She left the table and moved away, small heels tapping crisply. Grat Mallory gave a muffled curse and stared straight ahead, eyes moiling.

In a blue, long-running dusk Sheriff Bill Hammer rode a tall and weary grulla horse into Mineral and turned in at Jerry Pine's livery barn. Hoot McCall, a little gaunt and carrying his left shoulder with some stiffness, was back on his stage route, which left Jerry Pine free to get about his own business again. Jerry took the reins of Hammer's mount and ran a hand across the animal's sweaty flank.

"Must have been journeying, Bill."

"Canyon City," said Hammer.

"How'd you find things?"

"Quiet. Good bronc, this one. Deserves a rubdown, Jerry."

At the hotel Bill Hammer cleaned up, had supper, and then, with a cigar going, went along the street to where a light glowed in Burt Statler's office. Statler was cleaning up a little desk work and he waved Hammer to a chair.

"Be right with you in a couple of minutes, Bill. Just as soon as I make sure all the periods and commas are in the right place in this last paragraph." He grinned. "Such things count in this business, you know."

"Along with a lot of big words," murmured Hammer dryly. "Me, I never could see why you lawyers always have to clutter up some simple statement with so much jawbreaking, high, and fancy language."

Statler chuckled. "Got to make it sound important, Bill."

Hammer slouched deep in his chair, letting the weariness of a long day slide out of him. The smoke of his cigar curled upward and he watched it with half-closed eyes. A quiet man, capable, shrewd, and tenacious.

Statler finished with his reading, tucked the document away in his desk, leaned back. "Shoot, Bill. What's on your mind?"

Hammer dusted the ash from his cigar. "The day Bunch Grass was sold, the sale was held right in this office, wasn't it?"

"That's right. I'd met Styles. He asked me if he could conduct the sale here and I told him to help himself."

"You were here all the time, Burt? While the sale was going on and after, when Mallory paid Styles the cash?"

"Right here." Statler nodded. "In fact, I witnessed the receipt Styles gave Mallory."

"Fine! Then you saw what Mallory paid off with?"

"I did. He paid in currency—nice, new crisp stuff. In bundles of twenties that still had the Federal Reserve wrappers on them."

A gleam quickened in Bill Hammer's eyes. "Brand-new twenty-dollar bills. Well—well!"

Statler fixed the sheriff with a sober scrutiny. "You've picked up a hot lead, Bill?"

Hammer nodded. "I think so. Yes, I think so. Burt, none of this is to go an inch past your lips!"

"You can count on that, of course." Then, after a

moment of grave silence, Statler added, "I liked Jack Styles. A good, sound man. I think I could stand in at the hanging of those who killed him and come away with good appetite. Any other way I can help, just holler."

When Stack Portland opened his bank the next morning, Sheriff Bill Hammer was first to come through the door. "Got time for a word in private, Stack?"

The banker led the way into his small private office, closed the door. "Let's have it, Bill."

From an inside pocket Hammer brought out four crisp, new twenty-dollar bills. "Could you have these traced in any way, Stack? I mean the bank they came out of, and when?"

"Perhaps. Why?"

"Let me ask you this first," said Hammer. "Do you turn much new currency loose from this bank in twenty-dollar denomination?"

"A little. But not in any large amount lately, if that's what you mean."

"That's what I mean, Stack. Now, how would you go about tracing these bills?"

The banker took the four twenties, studied them a moment. "From the same series," he murmured. "This shouldn't be too hard. I can get in touch with the Federal Reserve and with some of the other banks round about. I think I can get an answer for you, Bill. May take a week or two."

"That's all right." Hammer nodded. "You can't rush a thing of this sort—not when you have to be dead sure. I'll leave the bills with you, Stack. Take care of them. They could be important evidence."

8. The Ways of Men

It was saddle work from dawn to dark. The trails of men and cattle crossing and recrossing, the range, as Cleve Fraser had put it, being tidied up. Brands being hazed back to their proper range after the scattering effect of the big winter drift. Long days and sunny ones, with spring heat giving promise of the summer's fierceness to come. Earth drying out and dust's amber haze lifting wherever men and cattle traveled. Soddy Joens getting his wish of sun on the back of his neck and the dust of the drag stinging his nostrils. And Soddy, as was his way, cussing it.

Cleve Fraser, moving up beside Soddy, heard and chuckled. "I can remember when you were wishing for this, Soddy."

Soddy blinked through the dust. "That's a fool man for you," he grumbled. "Never satisfied. Got one thing and he wants somethin' else. A man is God's dumbest critter. Grinds his life away for things he ain't got and don't need. Works himself to the bone to get somewhere, and when he arrives wishes he was somewhere else. A beef critter is smarter. Plumb satisfied with a bellyful of grass and a drink of water come morning and evening. Hunts some shade when it's hot and some sun when it's cold. Outside of that, the hell with it. Man ain't got that much sense."

They were bringing in a little gather from the far western reaches of Stony Creek's big bend. Fraser had left this chore to the last, and when this was done, he'd be ready to start his herd moving into the Sentinels.

Three men came riding in from the east: Pete Jackson, Jim Lear, and Pitch Calvin, who rode for Lear. Fraser swung away from the cattle and lifted an arm in greeting.

"Gentlemen! Looking for something, or just traveling?"

Pete Jackson's growl threw a shadow over Fraser's cheerful words. "Going to start looking for something damn quick! Cow thieves, Cleve—damn, stinking cow thieves. Want you to join in with us."

Fraser's eyes pinched down slightly and took on a shine of reserve. "No sign of such around here," he said tersely.

"Not around here, maybe," snapped Jim Lear in his waspish way. "But over in our country there's plenty of it. We're losing stuff all the time. And there's going to be some necks stretched!"

"Yeah?" murmured Fraser. "Whose?"

"Rustlers, of course," squalled Lear angrily. "Dammit, Fraser, this ain't no joking matter. What's wrong with you, man? Ain't you interested in stamping out this cussed thieving?"

Fraser built a casual cigarette, his glance going over these men. Jim Lear, stringy, shriveled, miserly, with a rodent's meanness in his faded eyes and a waspish cruelty in his heart. Pitch Calvin, slow-minded, heavy-bodied, thick-hided enough to stand for the acid bite of Lear's tongue, whereas a more self-respecting man would long ago have told Lear off and drawn his time.

And then Pete Jackson, more of a man than either of

the others, perhaps, but still a poor and soiled deck. Frowsy, unkempt, run over at the heels. Fraser could never remember seeing Pete Jackson when he didn't look like he'd just come in from a six months' drive across country where soap and water and a razor had never been heard of. At close range the man stank of stale sweat.

"Long as you ask," said Fraser finally, "yes, I want to see any rustling stopped. But not by any on-the-spot necktie parties arrived at by snap judgment. Bill Hammer is riding this range now. He's the man to see about any rustling problems."

"Hah!" snorted Pete Jackson. "Hammer couldn't catch butterflies. What's he done about them stage holdups? Not a thing. All he does is chase his tail in a circle. We leave it up to him we'll be rustled off the earth. Not me. This is one chore I handle my own way. And it could come rough!"

"Used to be a time when you seemed pretty salty about this yourself, Fraser," complained Lear. "How's it happened that you've softened down and become so righteous?"

"Why," murmured Fraser, "it could be that I've grown older and wiser. Anyhow, you got your answer."

Jim Lear stared at him, anger pulling his narrow face to a point. Lear rasped, "Hell with you!" Then he swung his horse and spurred away, Pitch Calvin following, riding heavy in his saddle. Pete Jackson hesitated, as though to argue further, then shrugged and lifted his horse to a run.

Fraser watched them for a little way, his face showing

126

a bleak contempt. Cattlemen they might be and, in a certain sense, neighbors. But he doubted if any of them had ever known a truly generous impulse in all the run of their lives, and as for liking them, he could not.

When Fraser dropped in behind the gather again, Soddy Joens asked, "What did them three greasy jiggers want?"

"Still whooping it up about rustler trouble. Wanted me to join in on a cow-thief hunt."

Soddy wangled a corner off a plug of tobacco, rounded the cud with pursed lips, then spat. "They would. But me, I'd hate to have to eat at one sitting all the veal meat Jim Lear and Pete Jackson have slipped their irons on when the real owner wasn't around."

"Soddy," accused Fraser, "you're a bitter man."

Soddy's lips quirked slightly. "Could be. But I figure I know which side of a card the spots are on."

The long, running shadows of sundown lay across the land by the time they got the gather pushed into the main herd which Happy Harte and Big Bob Scanlon were holding. Happy and Big Bob had a meager camp set up by a Stony Creek riffle and Soddy swung in and dismounted there. But Fraser stayed in his saddle, rubbing a hand across a whisker-stubbled jaw.

Meeting up with Pete Jackson and Jim Lear and Pitch Calvin, and weighing the tenor of their talk, had thrown Fraser's thoughts into a channel which led him back to a promise he'd made Pio Cardenas, and about which he'd as yet done nothing. Now he spoke in sudden decision.

"Soddy, you and Happy and Bob stay along with the

herd and hold it together. I'm going to headquarters, clean up a bit, and then head for town. We could use an extra hand on the drive into the hills and I'll see if I can locate one—Danny Cope, maybe."

Soddy tipped a shrewd head. "Doubt he'll care for regular work. Miracle man, that crazy kid. Seems to have found the secret of living without working." Soddy's tone was dry but brushed with meaning.

Sundown had become dusk and dusk nearing full dark when Fraser rode in at Saber. He reined up abruptly. The kitchen windows glowed yellow with light and the tang of wood smoke was on the evening air. Over in the black shadow of the ranch house a horse shifted and whickered softly.

Fraser went swiftly from his saddle, crossed over, had a look through a window, then went to the kitchen door and pushed it open. It was Sherry Dane who gave a little exclamation and swung to face him. She gave a quick sigh of relief, a small smile touching her lips.

"Please, kind sir, don't jump at conclusions before you hear my story. I'm only going according to what I've heard."

"So? And what's that?"

"The well-known hospitality of the West. That the wayfarer never goes away hungry, even if the owner of the ranch is not around at the moment. I'm really hungry, and I was just going to help myself to a small bite of this and that. Have I read the signs wrong?"

The shadowed gravity of Fraser's face broke. "Not if you see to it that there's a small bite of this and that for two hungry people. As a cook, how do you rate?"

"Not the best, not the worst. I'll try hard."

"Fly to it, then. I got a bronc to unsaddle and a session with a razor coming up. I like my coffee black."

Sherry Dane laughed softly. "You are a very understanding man, Cleve Fraser. I like your kitchen. It smells of warm living."

Half an hour later they sat down at the table. Fresh from the razor, Fraser's face was rugged, dark bronze in the lamplight. Looking across at Sherry Dane, he was thinking of the several times in the past when Leslie Cormack had pulled this same surprise on him, taking over his kitchen at unexpected times and laying hot food before him when it was most welcome.

Only there was a complete and unstudied naturalness about such an event when Les managed it, while now there was something in the air that sent him retreating warily back into a shell of reticence.

Sherry eyed him narrowly. "You're really half-angry with me," she accused.

He shook his head. "I'm just wondering how you happened to get way over here."

"Simple enough. I got tired of just riding around the limits of Bunch Grass Basin, so I set out to explore. I found a trail and rode it, and here I am. I thought of the ride back to town with nothing to eat, so I got reckless."

"Your uncle is probably worried about now."

She shrugged lightly. "Uncle Pardee seldom worries. He's always sure. He's been staying regularly out at the new headquarters and he probably thinks I'm patiently cooling my heels in town. There's nothing for him to worry about, is there?"

129

She asked this with a studied artlessness, but there was a flash of hard and worldly wisdom showing briefly in her eyes. Fraser saw this, and his wariness increased, his face going masklike.

"Sheriff Bill Hammer says you're pretty enough to knock a man's eye out. There are characters in the country who never saw your kind of beauty before."

She considered this for a moment, then laughed. "You're suggesting that I shouldn't try and ride back to town in the dark?"

"Hardly," said Fraser, dryly curt. "You'll ride, and I'll be riding with you."

Again she showed that look of hard wisdom. "You sound like a very proper man, Mister Fraser." There was a thread of mockery in her tone now.

"Careful fellow, that's me," he said with some harshness.

A bleak and dismal disgust had suddenly swept over him. He saw this situation with complete clarity now. It hadn't just happened. There was a lie in this room right now, and it wasn't even a good lie. He thought of Les Cormack, of her fine and wholesome naturalness, of her candid honesty and fine sweetness. Any room was a better room for Les Cormack having walked through it. But this—this was tawdry.

It was, he thought somberly, always a jolt to lose your respect for someone you had previously admired. And why was it that some women were like they were while others were like they were?

Sherry Dane was watching him, suddenly aware that she had played her hand badly. She was trying to read his thoughts, but not getting all of them, not sure of them. The hardness in her eyes moved into her features, sharpening them, pinching the beauty from them. Frazer pushed back his chair, his meal unfinished.

"I'll go saddle up. We're traveling."

So now she understood everything. For the first time in her life she'd met a man who saw through her completely, read her deceptive worth, saw past her carefully studied beauty. She had maneuvered this thing as cleverly as she knew how and it was like dust on the floor. No man had ever drawn her like this big, rugged son of the saddle and though he stood in this small room with her, he was a million miles away.

Fury at him, fury at herself, began to grind in her. She came to her feet, her glance flaying him. Anger thickened her voice slightly. "The big man of the range. The noble fool!"

"Fool, maybe," said Fraser, "but never noble. I just don't like lies."

He moved toward the door. Still she lashed at him. "You'll be broken—pushed back into a clod's corner where you belong. Uncle Pardee—Grat Mallory— they'll—!"

He moved through the door into the night, wondering how he'd ever thought there was beauty in her. He went over to the corrals to pick up a fresh bronc, but before he could catch and saddle he heard her horse explode into a run and in the starlight saw her, small in the saddle, racing along the outtrail into the timber.

He leaned against the corral fence, building a smoke. He was suddenly weary and filled with a vast distaste of life. Town held no lure for him now. Any business he had there could wait until tomorrow. A man set up a code and lived by it until it became habit. Did it mark him as a fool or a wise man? A man might have to wait all his life for the answer to that.

The air was cool, moist with night's dewy breath. The world was very still except when, long after Fraser's cigarette had gone dead and cold in his lips, a timber wolf mourned, distant as a fading echo.

Shortly after sunup the next morning Cleve Fraser rode up to Shield and Cross headquarters. Les Cormack, cool and straight in gingham, was stripping snowy, dew-sweetened wash from a line, piling it into a big wicker basket. Leaving his saddle, Fraser walked over to her, thinking that whatever this girl did was done with a free, unconscious grace. Her hands, brown and slim and strong, were always deft. She smiled over her shoulder at Fraser, but there was a strange and shadowed reserve in her eyes.

"Go in and see if you can calm Dad down, Cleve. He's all in a stew over this and that."

Fraser nodded then, as she reached up for another piece of wash, started and stared fixedly. "Whoa up! Something is missing." He was looking at her left hand. Vance Ogden's ring was no longer on her finger.

"Yes," said Les evenly. "It's gone. It should never have been there. It was a mistake, right from the first."

Fraser's eye corners pinched down. "What did Vance say when you gave it back to him?"

"I didn't see him. I mailed it to him."

He looked at her gravely. "Sure you mean it, Les? A thing like this—"

"I mean it," she cut in, meeting his look squarely. "I hope you don't think me a light and flighty person, Cleve. But . . ." She shrugged and looked away. "It was as if I'd just suddenly awakened. And then I was so very, very sure that it had all been a mistake. I can't explain it any better, but that's how it is."

"Tough on Vance," Fraser observed slowly. "He's been taking a lot of bumpings in the past few weeks. And maybe they've not all been entirely his fault. Maybe some of the rest of us are to blame somehow. Yeah, this is going to be rough on the old boy—rough!"

"I don't think so," differed Les quietly. "I think he'll be relieved. Now there won't be a single thing to interfere with his poker playing. We'll not mention it again, please."

Alec Cormack was propped up in bed, fussing with some tally books laid out on the covers in front of him. He grunted crustily as Fraser came in. "Don't ask me how this cussed leg is. It hurts like billy hell and I'm as helpless as a broken-backed old goat. But what's worrying me right now is what I'm going to do for grass. I've done some adding and subtracting, and I come to only one answer, which is to cut my herd way down. Losing Bunch Grass to Mallory and his crowd is now really beginning to hurt."

"I got a pretty good answer to that, Alec," said Fraser. "There's a lot of grass up in the Sentinels I don't need. Throw your surplus up there for the summer."

"I will not!" rumbled Cormack. "Been expecting you

133

to come up with that offer. But I'm not riding on your generosity just because I didn't have brains enough to think ahead."

"Now," drawled Fraser, "you're being stubborn as well as ornery. What's a little grass among friends?"

Cormack peered at him from under frosty brows. "You got a wide back and a strong one, boy. But you can't pack every dithering fool on it just because he's a friend. Besides, if I did take you up—not that I'm going to, understand—what would Wilcoxon and Shurtleff and Jackson and Lear think about it?"

Fraser shrugged. "Not their affair. Besides, in a pinch they can all work east. Not the best range in the world out that way, but plenty of room. Different with you. You got Bunch Grass on one side of you and me on the other. You're like a frog in a rain pipe. You got to go up or down. Down's the desert and nothing there. Up is the Sentinels and summer range. Simple as that, Alec. So quit stewing and count on it."

From the Shield and Cross Fraser went on to town. The first person he saw was Sheriff Bill Hammer, taking his ease on Henry Poe's store porch.

"Lazy hairpin," drawled Fraser. "You figure to catch anything sitting here?"

Bill Hammer showed a faint, dry smile. "Man stays in one place long enough there's no telling what might come shagging by. What's new, cowboy?"

Fraser told of his meeting with Pete Jackson and Jim Lear. "They're all in a froth to hang somebody, Bill. Maybe if you'd have a cold-turkey talk with them they'd cool off."

Bill Hammer stared along the street with narrowed eyes. "Jackson and Lear are sudden sort of jiggers. I'll talk to them."

Fraser went over to Pio Cardenas's workshop. Pio was there, stamping out a design on the skirt of a new saddle. Teresa, the girl, was there, too, lithe, black-eyed, and with a flashing smile.

"Señor Cleve—look!"

She dangled a slim brown hand before him. A small diamond solitaire flashed. "Danny," she said. "Danny gave it to me."

Fraser had watched this girl grow out of tempestuous, headlong childhood into swift, maturing beauty. He was genuinely fond of her and now, though something cold and stark clicked inside him, he kept the feeling completely hidden. This child who had so suddenly became a young woman was full of an inner delight that shone out of her like warm sunlight.

"Youngster," he said, "that's great. Prettiest ring I ever saw. I'll have to congratulate Danny. Where is he?"

"He is gone on business," chattered the excited girl. "He will be back tomorrow, he said."

"Teresa," said her father, "Señor Cleve and I would talk together. You will go and help your mother with her work."

The girl danced out, singing. Pio Cardenas looked at Fraser with eyes full of stark misery. "You see?" he said.

"I've been slow keeping a promise I made you, Pio." Fraser nodded. "But now I will get about it."

"I would be so happy for them both if there was steady work behind it," said Pio. "But—" He stared at nothing for a moment, then attacked his work a trifle fiercely.

Henry Poe was alone in his store. To Fraser's question he nodded. "Yeah, I ordered that ring for Danny Cope. Cost the best part of two hundred. Why?"

"I'm fond of both those kids," answered Fraser carefully. "Danny will need a good job to support a wife. Think I got one lined up for him."

Fraser went out and Henry Poe stared after him. "You're a damn good man, Cleve," he murmured. "But you're not fooling me. I wondered where Danny got that much money myself."

In the High Front, Pipe Orr shook his head. "Don't know where you'd find Danny, Cleve. Him and Ogden pulled out of here a couple of hours ago."

Fraser went out and stood looking along the street, a cold and foreboding pressure building up inside him. Sheriff Bill Hammer was no longer in sight, but Jonas Cain was lounging on his hotel porch, a gaunt shoulder point hitched against a pole support. Fraser crossed over. "Seen Danny Cope around, Jonas?"

The hotelkeeper nodded. "Him and Ogden rode out sometime back along the Canyon City road. Cleve, I'm a contented and happy man again."

"How's that, Jonas?"

"That finicky, fussy Pardee Dane hombre and his niece are pulling out from under my roof. Going to live out at the new headquarters on Red Bank Crick. About time. I'd have wrung his cussed, complaining neck had he stuck around another week. Abbie's just as tickled as I am. Say, Hoot McCall was telling me that Pardee Dane's got another herd of white-faces coming in.

Looks like he's aiming to pour cows into Bunch Grass until they start leaking out the edges. Should that happen, what'll the rest of you fellers do?"

"Another of those bridges I haven't come to yet, Jonas."

The gaunt hotelkeeper spat. "I've a feeling somebody is going to have to cuff Mister Pardee Dane around before he turns human. You keep an eye on that feller, Cleve. Both him and his niece can stand watching, Abbie claims. She says there's considerable hussy behind that girl's pretty face, and Abbie is shrewd that way."

Fraser went back downstreet to his horse and left town as though heading for home. Instead, he rode a circle that brought him back into the Canyon City road a good mile east of Mineral. A glance at the road's dustiness told him all he wanted to know. The marks of two horses that had moved along it not too long before showed plainly. Well out from town those hoof marks left the road and turned up a wash. Fraser followed them.

It was a still and empty world, slow breathing under the sun's strong beat. Sweat beaded through the horse's hide and gathered against Fraser's hatband. But inside him that ominous cold of foreboding held.

He watched both sides of the wash, and when several miles along he saw fresh hoof marks climb up and out, put his mount to the same trail. Over east lay the tumbled spread of Chinquapin Roughs, blurred and swimming in heat haze. There was a long crest to be crossed, after which he came down into the reaching flats beside Grizzly Creek. The sign stuck to these flats and led into the timber that finally came reaching down.

Here the hoofmarks split, one set cutting to the left of a down-reaching ridge, the other set leading to the right. Fraser followed those to the left. They wound along the ridge's left flank, crossed a gulch, climbed to another ridge top. Here a number of little terraced benches began and the timber gave way to spreads of aspen swamps fed with water seeps. Here also were small grass meadows and here also were cattle.

And here also—was Danny Cope!

Danny was working slowly and carefully, cutting out half-a-dozen of the best critters in sight, bunching these and hazing them to the east. Brands were mixed, which seemed to bother Danny not at all. So Fraser, watching from the edge of the timber, knew the stark, ugly truth beyond all doubt. He rode quietly out and came up to within thirty yards of Danny before Danny came around fast in his saddle, consternation sweeping his face. He started for his gun.

"No!" rapped Fraser. "You'd never get there, Danny. Don't be a bigger fool than you have been!"

Fraser had his gun out and Danny was looking into the steady muzzle of it. Fraser spoke again, reading the trapped desperation in this kid's eyes. "Easy! I don't want to have to throw a slug into you!"

The first wild resolve faded from Danny's eyes and the taut lift of his shoulders went into a slump. He licked his lips, swallowed thickly, and mumbled, "All right, Cleve. You got me!"

Fraser rode up, knee to knee with him. He reached out and lifted Danny's gun. Danny folded his hands on his saddle horn, tried unsuccessfully to meet Fraser's eyes, then stared at the ground. Rage broke from Fraser in a cold torrent.

"You double damned fool of a kid! I've a notion to take a quirt and wear it out on you. How long did you think you could go on getting away with this sort of thing? A rustler—a cheap cow thief! You knew better."

Danny licked his lips again. "I wouldn't let myself think. It was easy money."

"Easy money!" Fraser's lips curled. "Back in town a proud and happy girl showed me a new ring on her finger. Tickled half out of her skin and singing like a bird. Easy money! Why, damn you, I ought to whip you until you couldn't crawl. Teresa would be proud of that ring, wouldn't she, if she knew what you did to get the money? And those good people, her father and mother. How many hearts were you out to break, anyhow?"

Danny's head jerked up. "I'm on the square with Teresa," he blurted hoarsely. "We were to be married."

"Sweet future for her," rasped Fraser, "married to a damn rustler!"

Danny's head sagged again. "When you're young . . . ! I wanted so bad to get her that ring, and then I needed a stake to get married on. You won't believe this, maybe, but I was figuring on a regular job after we were married, and a ride that was square and straight from then on."

Fraser went still, letting this thing build up while the silence lay flat and heavy. Danny seemed to be waiting for Fraser to say something, and the long silence wove a net of hopelessness about him. So finally Danny shrugged, and his head came up and his lips pulled thin and tight.

"I don't deserve a damn thing, Cleve. I'll take my medicine. What is it?"

"Look at me!" ordered Fraser.

Danny Cope had blue eyes and tawny hair. Blue eyes, young eyes, that held steady. Blue eyes now shadowed with a cold dread, but still held steady.

"All right," gritted Fraser, "here's your medicine. You're getting out of here, riding straight to my headquarters. You'll see Soddy Joens there. Tell him I've hired you on to help us work the summer herd. And that's what you're going to do—work! I'll work you until you can't stand up. I'll haze you and I'll rough you up. And I'll break your damned neck with my two hands if you ever again so much as look at another man's cattle with any other eyes but honest ones. I'll make a man out of you or I'll kill you. Now you know!"

Danny held the fierce, built-up glare of Fraser's glance with eyes that seemed to go a little blind from the pressure of feelings that churned and rioted within him. His throat worked, and he jerked his head around, and Fraser saw his shoulders work up and down spasmodically. It took a little time for the kid to get control of himself again, and then his voice was thick and shaky.

"I'll be at Saber when you get there, Cleve."

"All right," rapped Fraser. "Here's your gun. Get going!"

Danny rode away, west. Fraser watched him out of sight, and the fierceness in his eyes faded to a somber moodiness. Softly he growled, "Damn fool kid!"

Fraser turned and looked out past the eastern run of

the benches. His chore wasn't done yet and there was no telling what the second part of it could lead to. It wouldn't be a reckless but scared kid like Danny Cope that he'd find at the end of that other set of hoofprints. It would be a man who had once been his closest friend, a man who had somehow and for some reason gone off at a sudden tangent, leaving all solidity and sane balance, tossing aside all the fine things in life most men dreamed of possessing. It wasn't going to be easy, this chore, and even if a man guessed at the answer he couldn't foresee it.

Fraser stirred his horse to a faster gait, for there was a black mood growing in him. He left the benches and the aspen swamps, dropped into gulches and crossed ridges, and then, when he felt he was drawing close, he grew high and wary in the saddle, alertness pulled to a fine, hard edge in him.

Twice he stopped and listened intently, and always his glance was swinging, probing. The air was still and warm and full of the baked, resinous fragrance of pine timber. Things were wrong here—there was something crawling up his spine, gathering at the nape of his neck—a sensory something that tied him in a knot inside. A dread . . .

He crossed another gulch, another ridge, and halfway down the far side of it set his mount back on sliding haunches. Fraser stared at the ground and here, where there should have been one set of horse tracks, the ground was chopped with several sets. And all of them, beyond this small tangled area, led down the curve of the sloping ridge toward the flats of Grizzly Creek.

Words broke with a groaning roughness over Fraser's lips. "God! They've got him. They've got Vance!"

His biting spurs lifted his big dun horse into a smashing run, weaving through the timber, crashing through thickets of lesser stuff, clearing a deadfall in one soaring leap. A file of cattle, working down toward the creek waters, scattered like startled quail. And the dun tore on.

Horse and rider exploded from the last timber fringe, broke into the open of the creek flats. There was a willow thicket jutting out, and beyond that a clump of towering alders. Clear of the willows and wheeling nervously back and forth was a riderless horse with dragging reins. Fraser had seen that horse before, many times, with Vance Ogden riding it.

Fraser's face went gray and old.

The pound of the dun's hoofs reached startled ears, and a rider swung into the clear at the willow point. It was Pete Jackson, his gun half raised. As he recognized Fraser, his chin dropped and his gun lowered. Then Jackson seemed to catch himself, started to lift the gun again, but was slow. The speeding dun was close enough, and Fraser swung a clubbing gun, savagely. Jackson ducked just far enough to save himself from a crushed skull. As it was there was plenty in the blow to knock him headlong.

Fraser cut the dun on a dime beyond the willow point. A rider loomed right in front of him. Pitch Calvin. There was no chance to dodge. The racing dun crashed full into Calvin's horse and they all went down, Fraser landing clear but hard on his shoulder. He rolled over twice and came to his feet.

Within a yard of him Jim Lear sat his saddle, his pointed face blank and stunned with the surprise and mad fury of it all. He didn't say a word or make a move until Fraser reached for him. Then he yelled. "Fraser! No—no! Cleve, you don't understand! No!"

Fraser dragged him from the saddle, whirled him high in the air, and slammed him savagely to the earth, like he would have flung some noisome rodent. There was a shrill scream of fear in Lear's throat that broke off sharply as he crashed down. Then he lay there, moaning.

Fraser stood for a moment, rigid. This, he thought brokenly, had been easy—an outlet to the madness that convulsed him. But now—now he had to turn around and look! Did he have it in him to do so?

He came around slowly, stiffening and straightening. He looked.

Something swinging on a rope from that tallest alder. Something swinging, slowly spinning—spinning . . .

Vance!

Fraser stumbled forward, fumbling for his pocketknife, knowing it was too late.

9. The Long Arm

HE HAD THEM IN FRONT OF HIM, WITHIN THE ARC OF A couched and ready gun, and his bleak glance raked them, and the words that came across his taut and stiffened lips were savage and merciless.

"You are three damned, dirty dogs! From this day forward, whenever or wherever I meet up with you, I'll call you the same and worse. I'll kick you out of the company of decent men. I'll dare you to throw a gun, and I'll kill you if you try. I'll make you crawl. You hear me— crawl!"

Two of them were still on the ground, Pete Jackson and Jim Lear. Jackson was dazed and sick, staring up at Fraser with bleared and bloodshot eyes that were dull with hate. Fear was Jim Lear's greatest injury. His pointed face was pallid and sweating, his lips working nervously across his teeth. As long as he lived Jim Lear would never forget the strange terror that had engulfed him when Cleve Fraser tore him from his saddle and swung him high before smashing him down to earth.

Pitch Calvin bore no discernible injury; he had come out of the smashing collision as able as Fraser. But this man's thinking was heavy and slow, ponderous as his physical bulk. He was a stupid animal, slow to catch fire, slow to act. He had shambled around wordlessly, doing what Fraser ordered him to do. Now he moved to obey another order.

"Bring in—his horse!"

Vance Ogden's horse, after wheeling and milling uncertainly beyond the willows, had come nervously in to join with Fraser's dun and the other animals. The dun had been uninjured by the driving impact, but Pitch Calvin's mount moved with a limp.

Pete Jackson was still unable to get to his feet and stay there unaided, so Fraser used a savage toe on Jim Lear. "Get up and help Calvin. Tie Vance across his saddle— and carefully!"

Pitch Calvin was unmoved by this grisly chore, a man

utterly devoid of imagination. But Jim Lear was pallid and shaking all through it. Finally it was done. Fraser had collected the guns of these three and thrown them into the dark depths of a creek pool. Now his words lashed them again.

"Get moving! Get out!"

They had to help Pete Jackson to his feet, guide his stumbling steps, boost him into his saddle. But when they rode away, though the other two were silent, venom poured across Jackson's lips in unintelligible, half-formed curses.

They were gone, and the long creek flats lay empty, except for a stir of cattle here and there. Shadows were beginning to form, blue and flowing. More of the day had gone than Fraser realized. Time got away from a man under some conditions. The account of it and everything else could be lost and forgotten in a gust of wild, helpless frenzy that left a man weary beyond measure and drained dry of all measurable and definable emotion.

He picked up the reins of Vance Ogden's horse, stepped into his own saddle, and moved out.

Town in the first dusk. Yellow lights springing up beyond window and open door; the tang of wood smoke from evening fires a bland pungency in the evening air. Life going on for some, as it always had and always would. A few might pause long enough to know a thin regret and then, with the others, would move on down the trail, forgetting.

Fraser circled the edge of town on the north, coming up to the rear of Jerry Pine's livery corral. Here he left both horses and went in search of Bill Hammer. As he reached the street there was the clack of wheels and the creak of leather thorough braces as Hoot McCall came along with his stage, filling the street with a sense of movement, the breath of sweating horseflesh, and the bite of freshly stirred-up dust.

It had been a dry run in from Breed's junction, carrying nothing but the mail, so Hoot pulled up at the stable and Henry Poe came across the short interval and caught the mail sack as Hoot tossed it down. When Poe went back to his store, the snowy head of Stack Portland shone under the light of the store's hanging lamps as he, too, stepped in from the outer gloom. As Fraser started along the street he recognized the lean, smooth-striding figure of Bill Hammer coming from the hotel toward the store. He sent a short hail.

"Bill! Fraser. Want to see you."

Keen in such things, the sheriff recognized the flat emptiness in Fraser's tone, and his stride quickened as he angled over. "What is it, Cleve?"

"This way," said Fraser. They circled the livery barn. Fraser said, "It's Vance."

Bill Hammer swore in startled sharpness. "Tell me!"

Fraser did so, his words running on in a ragged monotony. "I got there just too late. He was dead when I cut him down," he ended.

"Jackson, Lear, Calvin—what about them? Cleve, you didn't?"

"No, I didn't gun them. Maybe I should have. Maybe, when I'm able to straighten out my thinking a little better, I'll hunt them down and do it anyhow. As it was,

I just roughed them around some. The slimy whelps! Who are they to take it upon themselves—?"

"But they must have caught him cold—red-handed, Cleve?"

"I guess—No, I know they did. I was trailing him myself. Just the same"

"I know," cut in Hammer quietly. "This sort of thing is bad."

"Bill, I want you to go after those three."

"For this, all I could do would be rawhide hell out of them," said Hammer. "Dragging them into court on a count like this wouldn't get us anywhere. Popular sentiment would be on their side. Oh, I know how you feel, Cleve, but to most he would be just a rustler, caught up with. It's one of those things, boy. In time you'll come to realize it. Here's what you should do. Head for the High Front and get outside a real slug of liquor. I'll get Jerry Pine to help me with things."

"No!" said Fraser harshly. "You and me, we'll take him in."

So they carried Vance Ogden into the stable, laid him down on the thick straw of an empty stall, and covered him with his own saddle blanket. Bill Hammer took Fraser by the elbow, steered him out to the street.

"Don't leave town until you see me again, Cleve. You and I may still make a ride tonight. I'll let you know."

Bill Hammer hurried over to Henry Poe's store. Presently he and Stack Portland came out together and went up to the bank, Portland unlocking the door and leading the way inside. Fraser saw none of this, for he'd gone over to the home of Pio Cardenas, where the family had just settled down to their evening meal. Maria Cardenas bustled about to set a place for Fraser, who shook his head.

"Thanks, but no, Maria," he said. "Some other time."

Fraser could feel Pio's glance holding on him almost breathlessly. Fraser forced himself to smile as he looked at the girl Teresa.

"Your boy friend won't be around for a while, Teresa. Danny's signed on with me for the summer. I'm taking him up into the Sentinels with me. But come fall we'll all dance at the wedding."

For a moment the girl showed dismay. Then, glancing at her ring, she smiled. "If I could see him but once more before he leaves, señor Cleve, I will be content." Her smile became a shy laugh. "And I will wish for the fall to hurry."

The warmth of this girl's fervor touched Fraser and in some strange way drove back the gray and bitter edge which had been consuming him. "I'll let him come in to see you before we leave," he promised.

Fraser swung his head, met Pio's eyes, and drew his full reward. Pio's voice shook just a trifle as he said, "You are my true and fine friend, señor Cleve."

Fraser went back to the street and prowled along it. The first blinding shock of this thing had passed. In all except the raw torment inside him he was the same man he'd always been. A piece had been chewed out of the past and relegated to the files of memory. Things to remember, things to try to forget. He wondered if the mind was like a photographic film, holding an impression forever? The impression of Vance, on that rope, swinging and slowly spinning . . . ?

Sheriff Bill Hammer's voice, crisp and driving, broke through the black depths of Fraser's musings. "Come on, Cleve. We ride, you and me!"

Hammer, just out of the bank, was hurrying across the street lying pale under the first stars. Fraser asked, "Ride where?"

"Vengeance is a word some people don't like," Hammer said mysteriously. "Yet the desire for it is a human thing. I promise you this—you'll not rate this ride wasted. Come on!"

Fraser got the dun, and Hammer saddled up one of Jerry Pine's stable string. The way led out of town, north and east. Fraser, wondering, finally sorted out the trail. They were headed straight for Jim Lear's Lazy L headquarters.

"I thought," said Fraser, "you said it would do no good to arrest them?"

"For what you think, no," answered Bill Hammer. "For what I think, yes. This will jar you, Cleve."

In time they picked up the lights of the place, lights as meager and stingy as Jim Lear himself. A rickety layout, with not a dollar spent for anything but the bare essentials. They came in quietly, left their horses back a piece, and closed in on foot. Bill Hammer pushed open the cabin door, and as he stepped in, laid his order flat and crisp.

"We'll play this hand steady!"

On a bunk in one corner Jim Lear sprawled, sucking on a thin cigarette. At the rough, bare board table Pitch Calvin was swabbing up some tin supper dishes. He stared heavily, slow in understanding this. But Jim Lear came up sitting, his pinched and pointed features beginning to work nervously as he looked at Fraser. The terror of the afternoon was still in this man.

"We caught him cold, Hammer," shrilled Jim Lear. "He was picking out the best of a little bunch of—"

"That's past," cut in Bill Hammer. "This is something else. Calvin. Ever see these before?"

Hammer took four twenty-dollar bills from a pocket, held them spread in his fingers. Pitch Calvin stared a moment, then said, "Money? Sure, I've seen money before. Why them?"

"These exact greenbacks got away from you in a poker game one night a while back, over a table in Canyon City," Hammer said. "I heard the story of that game and I bought these bills from the man who won them. With Stack Portland helping me, I find they are part of the sum of fifty thousand dollars drawn from the Mercantile Bank in Breed's Junction by Grat Mallory through the medium of a certified check for that amount, signed by Pardee Dane. Cleve, watch Lear! He's beginning to squirm!"

This was true. Jim Lear had drawn himself up into a taut, crouched bundle, his look that of a trapped animal. Desperation was a hard glare in his bleached and faded eyes.

"Of that fifty thousand dollars," went on Hammer, "Grat Mallory paid thirty-one thousand for the purchase of Bunch Grass Basin. When Jack Styles, who handled the sale for the government, was on his way out to Breed's junction by stage carrying the purchase price with him, the stage was held up by three men and Styles was murdered. Calvin, did you get a full third of that thirty-one thousand?"

"Pitch!" yelled Jim Lear, "keep your mouth shut. Don't say a word. They don't know—"

"I know you're damned worried about something, Lear," cut in Hammer coldly. "Cleve, we're going to look this place over and tear it plank from plank if we have to. Lear, you and Calvin get over against that wall. Face it and put your hands against it—high up. Move!"

There was a reluctance with which Lear left his bunk and a final furtive smoothing movement with his hand which Fraser did not miss. As Lear and Calvin faced the wall under Bill Hammer's bleak authority, Fraser stepped up to the bunk.

"Got a hunch this might be a good place to start looking, Bill," he said.

Fraser didn't find it among the blankets, but he did find it inside the end of the grass-stuff bunk pad. Bundles of currency, crisp and new. Head twisted, watching over his shoulder, Jim Lear groaned thinly.

"Hoot McCall didn't die, did he? No, he didn't die. You can't blame me for worse than that. Pete Jackson killed Styles . . ."

They let Lear talk himself out. He was almost groveling at the last. Even the heavy, thick-witted Pitch Calvin stared at him with scorn and contempt.

"You'd have thought he'd found a better hiding place for it than that, Cleve," said Hammer.

"He's a rat, isn't he?" Fraser shrugged. "And it's rat nature to haul loot into their nest."

Pitch Calvin, stolid, phlegmatic, understanding in his own way that the jig was up, showed them where he'd stashed his share.

An hour later they rode up to Pete Jackson's headquarters. Jim Lear and Pitch Calvin were tied in their saddles, ankles to cinch rings, wrists to saddle horns. There was no light in Pete Jackson's cabin.

"You watch these two, Cleve," said Bill Hammer. "I'll gather in Jackson."

"In his way, stronger stuff than these, Bill," cautioned Fraser. "He could be dangerous. Watch yourself!"

"I always watch myself," murmured Hammer dryly.

Bill Hammer went up quietly, knocked at the door. He knocked three times before he got a hard and muffled answer.

"Name yourself!"

"Bill Hammer, Jackson. I want you!"

"Not for helping string a damn rustler. You can't hold me for that, Hammer."

"We'll see. Coming in, Jackson!"

Bill Hammer drew his gun and kicked the door wide.

Jackson cursed harshly. "You don't have to knock the place down. All this fuss over a stinking rustler. Wait'll I get a light going."

A match flared weakly, touched a lamp wick, and a thin yellow glow took over the cabin. Pete Jackson was in his underwear, just out of his blankets. He had a crude bandage on his head and the cabin smelled of whisky. He stood with his left side toward the door. His right hand was hidden.

Stepping full into the doorway, Bill Hammer said,

"Jackson, I want you for the murder of Jack Styles! You fool! Don't try it!"

But Pete Jackson did try it. That hidden right hand snaked into view and there was the blue of gun steel in it.

Sheriff Bill Hammer shot twice, from the hip. Pete Jackson shot once, as he was falling, driving a gout of splinters from the floor.

"No, Cleve, Les isn't here. She's off riding somewhere. I declare, I never saw that girl so restless as she's been lately. She just can't stay around the house any more. Come in, boy. Breakfast's over hours ago, but I'll have some coffee ready in a jiffy—"

Sarah Cormack was a vigorous upstanding woman, active and energetic despite the silver that was beginning to brush her hair. Kindliness lay in her and a love for her family and her ranch-house home came out of her in a warming glow.

Cleve Fraser spun his hat in his hands and tried to find the right words. "I'm glad Les isn't here, Mother Cormack. I was afraid she would be, and I'd rather she'd hear it from you than from me. You'll understand how to say it better."

He saw the swift anxiety leap into Sarah Cormack's eyes. "Boy, there's a look about you. You're weary, and there's something in your eyes . . ."

"Alec will have to know too," said Fraser. "I'll tell you both."

Sarah Cormack led the way into her husband's room. Alec Cormack stirred restlessly in his bed and sent up his barking growl. "Cleve, what's this about another herd of white-faces coming in? That damn Pardee Dane must be figuring—"

"Hush, Alec!" cut in Sarah Cormack. "Cleve has something else to tell us."

From beneath jutting, frosty brows Alec Cormack peered at Cleve. Then he said, with keen intuition, "It's Ogden—Vance Ogden?"

Slowly Fraser nodded. "That's right, Alec. He's gone." Sarah Cormack gave a soft little cry, and her hands came together, twisting.

A trifle heavily, Alec Cormack said, "Dead?"

"Yes. Pete Jackson, Jim Lear, and that rider of Lear's, Pitch Calvin—they caught him rustling. They—lynched him."

Sarah Cormack whirled and hurried from the room. Alec Cormack plucked at the bedcovers with aimless fingers, while a fierceness built up in his eyes. His voice came out in a low, hard rasp.

"The damned, vicious whelps! For that they should be run out of the country. When I'm able to be up and around again I'll take a stand for that. Cleve, he was— rustling?"

"Yes, Alec."

"They still had no right. I'll make them bleed. I'll see to it that they—"

"No need, Alec. That's already happened."

"How? You mean that you—"

"I was there. Bill Hammer handled things. He got his three men who held up the stage and killed Jack Styles. Jackson's dead—he tried to make a fight of it. Lear and

Calvin go out to Breed's junction to stand trial. With the law reading as it does for that sort of crime, neither of them will ever be back. I guess you could say that things are pretty well evened for Vance."

"So!" growled Cormack. "They were the three! That isn't at all as I figured it would be. Yet, now that you tell me this, it's so damn logical. They were there, at the sale. They knew the amount of money paid. They knew Styles would be taking it out on the stage with him. And as I recall, Jackson and Lear didn't stay around town long after the sale was over. Went off together, on some excuse or other. The mangy crooks! Whining about losing a few cows, yet all the time—A-argh!" Cormack swung a clenched fist in a short gesture.

There was silence, while the fierceness died out in the old cattleman. Then, with brooding heaviness, he asked, "How could a man go all to pieces so suddenly?"

"Something I've been trying to figure out, Alec," Fraser answered wearily.

"Looking back across the years," said Cormack slowly, "I can recall a couple of others who went the same way. They stood up to life just so long. Then, suddenly, it seemed to whip them and they let go all holds and began to slide. Looks like Vance was one of such, Cleve."

"I guess," said Fraser, "that's as good an answer as any, Alec." He shrugged and moved to the door. "I'll be watching Pardee Dane and his herds and I'll let you know."

Sarah Cormack stood at a window near the ranch-house door. She was staring at nothing, dabbing her eyes occasionally with her apron. Fraser stood beside her awkwardly, not knowing what to say.

"If it only could have been in any other way, boy," she said in muffled tones.

He would be thirty on his next birthday, but Mother Cormack always called him "boy." She always would.

He touched her shoulder briefly and went out.

Things were active at Saber headquarters. In front of the saddle shed Happy Harte was sorting and checking over sawbuck packsaddles, ropes, tarps, and other pack gear. Happy was whistling contentedly. He had a trick of putting out a fluting, birdlike warble, and it was a pleasant, cheerful sound.

In one of the corrals Big Bob Scanlon was cold shoeing several of the cavvy broncs and Danny Cope was there, helping him. Soddy Joens was stacking grub items on the narrow porch of the ranch house and came sauntering over as Cleve Fraser rode up. Soddy jerked his head toward Danny Cope.

"Made up your mind kinda sudden there, didn't you?"

"Figured we could use an extra man," said Fraser briefly. "The kid's got the makings of a good hand."

"Um!" Soddy grunted enigmatically. He looked at Fraser keenly. "What knothole did you get dragged through?"

While he unsaddled, Fraser gave Soddy the whole story, tersely blunt. Soddy blinked.

"Didn't I tell you, Cleve, that Jackson and Lear and Calvin had coyote sign all over them? Well, Bill Hammer is one long, shrewd arm of the law for my money." Soddy considered for a moment, then twitched his head again toward Danny Cope. "When the story gets around there may be some who'll ask questions about him."

"He's riding for and with us," answered Fraser. "If they say too much, kick their teeth in."

Again Soddy blinked. "Just so, Cleve."

Knowing that Soddy would see to it that the others got the word, Fraser went into the ranch house, pulled off his boots, and stretched out on his bunk. Here it was warmly still. Through the open window the resin-scented air poured with steady comfort. He hadn't slept a wink the night before. But now, for some reason, he was easier inside, more relaxed. Maybe, in telling others about Vance he'd lightened the load on himself. Which was a queer way to feel about it, but it could be so. He was pondering this theory when sleep took him.

The day had just about run out when he awakened. He shaved, had a wash, and went out, the lines in his face softened somewhat and much of the old spring back in his muscles. Danny Cope was over at the corrals, brushing down his horse. Every move Danny made was mechanical.

Fraser hooked his arms on the corral fence. Danny looked at him, stark misery in his blue eyes. "You should have let them have me too. If Vance deserved it, so did I."

"Wouldn't have happened to Vance if I could have got there in time. Kid, that's a closed book. Never open it again. Care to say where you and Vance were heading with those cows?"

Slowly Danny shook his head. "That would make me

lower than I am. Which is a poor answer to give you, Cleve, after the break you've given me. But that's the way it will have to be.

Fraser nodded. "Had to ask. But I'd have thought the less of you if you'd told. Saw Teresa in town. She's happy over your new job and willing to wait until fall to get married, providing she can see you once more before you head into the hills with me. So you might as well head for town. Don't be too late getting back. Busy days ahead."

Danny slugged his startled bronc in the ribs with a clenched fist—not too hard. "Vance got the rope," he choked. "I get this. The world's crazy!"

But half an hour later, when Danny rode down the town trail, he was high and eager in his saddle. Watching him go, Fraser smiled grimly. "Come fall, kid," he murmured, "you'll be all right."

The outfit was just sitting down to supper when Art Wilcoxon and Dab Shurtleff rode in. Talk was idle and of little moment until the meal was done and Fraser led the way over to the ranch house through the serene blue dusk.

"Just right out here," said Art Wilcoxon, hunkering down on the porch edge. "Get it off your chest, Dab."

"After what's happened," said Shurtleff in his blunt and heavy way, "a man gets to wondering just who's crooked and who's straight in this damned world. The Jackson, Lear, and Calvin part don't surprise me too much somehow. But the rest puts me back on my heels. Art and me been wondering if Ogden was long riding alone. Him and young Cope were together a lot around town."

"Danny Cope," said Fraser clearly, "is my man. Drawing wages from me and chousing my cattle. He heads into the hills tomorrow with Saber."

"Recent thing, ain't it, his signing on with you?"

"Maybe, but still a fact."

Neither Wilcoxon nor Shurtleff missed the significant inflection in Fraser's tone. Wilcoxon said mildly, "Guess that answers it."

Dab Shurtleff, not quite so readily or willingly, finally nodded. "Yeah," he growled, "guess it does. We'll consider that page turned. But what about Pardee Dane and all the cattle he's bringing in? Maybe you got an answer to that, too, Fraser?"

"I was halfway figuring on riding over tonight and asking Dane about it," said Fraser. "He's the one who should know. What do you fellows think?"

"Right with you," said Art Wilcoxon, getting to his feet. "High time we quit guessing and got at some facts."

10. Gathering Storm

IN A HEADQUARTERS OFFICE THAT SMELLED OF NEW lumber and newer paint, Pardee Dane sat at ease, a freshly lighted perfecto drawing free and fragrantly between his lips. Across the desk from him was Grat Mallory, stained with the marks of hard riding.

In a chair in a corner Sherry Dane was curled, feet tucked beneath her, examining her faultlessly kept fingernails with brooding preoccupation. Somehow she looked older than usual, and a little weary. In her dark eyes was a strange uncertainty, as though life had held certain values which she had never considered before and now, suddenly recognizing them, and seeing them as desirable, found them tantalizingly beyond her reach.

Grat Mallory, after watching her guardedly for a moment, turned to Pardee Dane. "We've cut the herd for a thousand head of the sturdiest. They're ready to go. Still want to go through with it?"

"Of course," said Pardee Dane crisply. "There's no sounder course than our original strategy. Once we get control of the Garden and the other high meadows of the Sentinels, we can begin to spread our elbows in any direction we desire. There's no place for the opposition to go but out. By fall we should have things pretty well sewed up. Not having any qualms, are you, Grat?"

Mallory shrugged. "Just wanted to be sure that you realize what is sure to come. One hell of a fight. Fraser's no fool, and he's tough. The others, Cormack, Wilcoxon, and Shurtleff—they'll back his hand because there's nothing else they can do."

"I see no reason to expect any more trouble than we had in Ruby Valley, for instance," said Dane. "I recall plenty of bluff and bluster thrown our way there, but when the chips were on the table the blusterers backed down."

"Sure they did—there." Mallory nodded. "But here things are different. The outfits we had to buck in Ruby Valley and on Bidwell Plains, too, for that matter, had nothing left to put up a fight about, once we bought the government grass from under them. You might say most of them were transients, staying on for government grass alone. We'd bought that, all legal and according to Hoyle. The law stood behind our claim. Realizing that, the other outfits moved out peaceably enough."

"A comparable situation exists right here," said Dane.

"No, it doesn't," differed Mallory. "The main outfits here are dug in, have been here a long time on range that is really theirs. Even after losing out on Bunch Grass they can, by cutting down their herds some, still get by. They won't scare easy or bluff easy. They'll fight. And if they pool their strength, they can make it plenty tough."

"Grat," accused Pardee Dane sarcastically, "I believe you're losing your nerve."

Mallory flushed, and his eyes began to moil. "Once and for all, Mr. Dane, let's drop that kind of talk. I've never let you down yet and I'm not going to start now."

Their eyes locked, and it was Pardee Dane who looked away. "Consider it unsaid, Grat."

"Fair enough," said Mallory. "We'll go ahead with the plan as you wish. But you better get used to gun smoke, for you're going to smell it. One thing, we won't have Bill Hammer in our hair. He's going out to Breed's junction with Lear and Calvin. There was an angle that sure fooled me—those who pulled the stage holdup, I mean."

Pardee Dane smiled cynically. "That affair confirms my belief that there are few thoroughly honest people."

Outside, spur chains tinkled, and a knock sounded at the office's outer door.

"See who it is and what they want," said Pardee Dane.

Mallory opened the door. It was Chess Breshear, and he said, "Visitors. Fraser, Wilcoxon, and Shurtleff. Shall

I have the boys let them in?"

"What do they want?" Mallory asked.

Breshear jerked a nod toward Pardee Dane. "Say they want to have a talk with him."

Pardee Dane said, "Send them in."

Sherry Dane slipped from her chair and left the office quietly by an inner door.

Pardee Dane looked at Grat Mallory triumphantly. "When they begin coming to us, it means their nerve is running out."

"Maybe," said Mallory dryly. "But I wouldn't count on it."

Fraser was the first to enter, then Dab Shurtleff, with Art Wilcoxon in the rear. Wilcoxon closed the door, stood with his back to it. Pardee Dane settled down behind his desk, looked at them. "Sorry I haven't enough chairs in here for all. But perhaps your business with me won't take long. I hope not, for I'm very busy getting—"

"Stow that!" said Dab Shurtleff bluntly. He looked Pardee Dane up and down. "Our business will take as long as it takes. And you'll listen."

Pardee Dane's hands pressed white on the desk top and his cold eyes glinted in the lamplight. He wasn't used to being spoken to in this manner. "Careful!" he warned. "I can call my men and—"

"And I can gut shoot you and watch you kick before they ever get here," cut in Shurtleff, rough and harsh as always. "Come down off your high perch. If you figure you're wearing a crown it's all in your imagination. You got all the earmarks of a damn crook to me. And I never used soft words on a crook."

Fraser saw the bleak fury build up in Pardee Dane's face, sending little muscular quivers across his precise features. Dane's lower features seemed to cave in as his lips grew almost invisible under pressure. "Have your say," he choked, "and then get out!"

"It's about cattle," said Fraser. "You're bringing in more than Bunch Grass can handle for any length of time. Question is, do you intend to ruin a great piece of range by overgrazing, or do you figure to let some of the cattle spill over the borders of Bunch Grass? The first is your business, for you own Bunch Grass. But the second possibility is our business. So, we want to know."

"That's right," seconded Shurtleff, "we want to know."

"My plans and my affairs are my own," gritted Dane. "Does that answer you?"

"Under ordinary circumstances, yes," said Fraser. "But these are very strange circumstances. You'll have to say more."

Pardee Dane's glance ran over the three of them. "I discuss my plans only with whom I choose. I do not choose to do so with you. You can leave the same way you came."

Dab Shurtleff began to growl, but Fraser stopped him with a hand on his arm. "We're not so coy about our plans, Dane. Frankly, we don't trust you. We think your ambitions are outsize. We feel that you've got this thing figured as another Ruby Valley or Bidwell Plains affair. We suggest you change your mind. Trouble ahead if you don't."

"You can't stand in my own ranch house and threaten me," rapped Dane. He had got a grip on himself again and the old, cold mask had taken over. "I don't scare."

"Not trying to threaten, not trying to scare," said Fraser. "Just telling you, that's all. You'll get what you ask for." With that Fraser turned and looked at Grat Mallory. "This is for you, personally."

Grat Mallory was playing the part of a slightly bored listener to it all. But the pinched, hard shine in his black eyes told of his inner alertness. "All that Mr. Dane says goes for me, too, Fraser."

"This," said Fraser harshly, "is something else. Yesterday a man who'd been my good and long time friend was lynched as a rustler. I won't try to analyze the breakup inside him that made him slip as far as he did. But this I know. It started after he came to know and play poker with you. He went down the slide himself, but you greased it for him. He touched you and went bad, Mallory."

Mallory shrugged. "Ogden knew what he was doing. He was over twenty-one. He must have liked it that way. Why should you kick?"

"Because," rapped Fraser, "I don't think Vance would have ended as he did if you hadn't given him a damn big push in that direction. Yeah, Mallory—he touched you and went bad. I'm never going to forget that. I don't believe this range will ever be big enough to hold you and me at the same time."

Mallory's smooth, dark face tightened and his glance flickered around before coming back to Fraser. "A stacked deck," he said evenly. "I don't bite."

"This is an extra thought and all Fraser's," growled Dab Shurtleff. "Ogden was his friend, Mallory—not mine. So don't let me and Wilcoxon hold you back."

"A stacked deck," said Mallory again.

Art Wilcoxon said, "We could stay here all night and end up the same place."

Fraser nodded and moved to the door. "Come on!"

They went out, he and Wilcoxon and Shurtleff. They went swiftly to their horses, swung up. Round about them in the dark were men, Chess Breshear, Loop Scarlett, and others. Fraser knew they were there, though he could not see them. But there was no hostile move. When they had put a couple of hundred yards between them and the headquarters, Art Wilcoxon let out a long breath.

"If Mallory or Dane had opened that door and hollered, things could have turned interesting, Cleve."

"Maybe. But they're not worked up to that point yet."

"Kind of pushing the personal angle with Mallory, weren't you?" growled Shurtleff. "What was the idea?"

"You heard what I said," was Fraser's brief reply. "That was the idea."

Shurtleff grunted. "Hard enough trying to prop up a live man. No point in doing the same for a dead one, no point at all."

Fraser did not answer. Dab Shurtleff had his good points, but he was a man whose life was guided by a hard, unimaginative practicality. He could never understand how it was about Vance.

"Well, anyhow, I think we made our point clear," said

Wilcoxon. "Dane knows what the future holds if he gets out of bounds."

Back in the Rafter X office, Pardee Dane was pacing his anger off, up and down, up and down. "The damned nerve of them!" he exploded. "Trying to threaten me in my own bailiwick. They'll get their answer. Fraser goes first and then that damned, rough-tongued slug of a Shurtleff!"

Grat Mallory's eyes held a sardonic glint. "Still think it's going to be as simple as Ruby Valley or Bidwell Plains?"

The inner door opened, and Sherry Dane stepped through. No man could have correctly read the thoughts which lay behind the still brooding of Sherry's eyes, for her thoughts and emotions were so jumbled she could not fully understand them herself. She spoke simply.

"I listened. I think you would be smart, Uncle Pardee, to be satisfied with what you have."

Pardee Dane swung on her testily. "Good God, girl, don't tell me that you, too, see things about this fellow Fraser that I can't—that he's too big, too tough?"

Sherry shrugged. "Could be a woman's intuition at work."

"My dear," said Pardee Dane, with some acid, "suppose you tend to your own small affairs and let me manage the bigger ones." He whirled on Grat Mallory. "We put that herd into the Sentinels, into this Garden spot that Fraser's so proud of. That's final and settled!"

If Leslie Cormack had been restless before, she was doubly so now. She didn't want to go to town, for she knew people would look at her and be wondering about her thoughts concerning Vance Ogden. And she couldn't stay in the house. She had to ride and ride, and she did just that, going no place in particular, just so she was out and moving somewhere.

She'd given up trying to analyze her feelings over the news of Vance Ogden's death. When her mother had put comforting arms about her and given her the story, Leslie's first reaction had been a sort of shocked numbness. The cruel ignominy of such an end had left her stunned and sickened.

She had wept some, but more because of tarnished memories than from any dire sense of loss. And this had puzzled her and made her angry at herself. It offended her sense of propriety that something which had once been so great in her life should so suddenly have become of lesser moment. Was she shallow, callous? Just what sort of a person was she, anyhow?

How, she wondered, was Cleve Fraser taking it? She knew his deep, headlong faithfulness toward his friends; she knew how much he'd thought of Vance. Suddenly she wanted to see Fraser above all else, see him and talk to him and perhaps win from him an answer concerning her own questions about herself. Back across the years Cleve had somehow always understood. . . .

She had ridden as far as Stony Creek and had crossed it before she realized that as far as she could see across Saber's big-bend winter range there was not a single cow critter in sight. Which meant only one thing. The Saber herd had already started up into the Sentinels, on its way to summer range. And that meant she'd find no one at Saber headquarters. But she went on just the same, and then sat her saddle in grave silence as she looked around the still and deserted headquarters.

She knew a swift surge of regret because Fraser had headed into the hills without a good-by to her; it was the first time this had ever happened. But just as swiftly she understood why he had not. It would have been impossible for them to meet and talk without the shadow of Vance standing before them, and that was something which would have hurt both of them until time had softened matters and given some comforting philosophy a chance to take form. Les was musing on this when she heard the tap of approaching hoofs. She turned and went still in her saddle. It was Sherry Dane riding in.

For a moment Les knew a stir of almost anger; it was as though this girl from the outside was intruding into something that was none of her affair—into a fabric of the past that had known its great and good moments and which belonged to just the three of them, to Cleve Fraser and Vance Ogden and herself. Then Les took hold of herself and called on her old dignity. She managed a fairly pleasant greeting, despite the mixed-up and half-wistful turmoil inside her.

"Nobody home," she said. "Which means that Cleve and his crew have started into the mountains with the cattle."

This was a different Sherry Dane than Les had ever seen before. The usual bright manner was missing. She was grave and preoccupied and her eyes were shadowed. She spoke slowly.

"I'm sorry to hear that. I was hoping to see Mr. Fraser.

I've important word for him. I—I think it is important."

Leslie was startled. "Important—how? If you'd care to tell me it can be arranged for a rider to carry the word to Cleve."

Sherry considered for a moment, then nodded. "Very well. Here is the word. Rafter X is about to start around a thousand head of cattle up into the Sentinels. The destination is to be some place called the Garden. There will be a large force of riders with the herd. Grat Mallory will be in charge. The riders have orders to shoot their way through any opposition that arises. I would like to know that Mr. Fraser has been warned of that."

Les Cormack stared at her, while anger lifted swiftly. "Rafter X cattle—in the Garden? Why, that's Cleve Fraser's best piece of summer range. That's range piracy. It's what everyone has feared—that Bunch Grass would not be enough to satisfy Pardee Dane. He's out to do what he has done in other places, which is drive other cattlemen out—hog their range—!"

Sherry Dane met Les Cormack's flaming glance very steadily. "That is what I'm afraid of," she admitted. "And I don't want it to happen, not to Cleve—Mr. Fraser. That is why I was bringing him word, hoping to warn him."

Les Cormack's turmoil of feeling did not lessen. Here was a new note, and it shook her. This girl's concern for Cleve Fraser. Why? What was behind it? For the life of her Les could not keep a chill stiffness out of her next words.

"You hardly know Cleve Fraser. Your concern seems strange."

"Doesn't it!" Just a hint of a weary smile touched Sherry's lips. "Only another woman could possibly understand it. At first I couldn't understand it myself. Now I do—so very well. You see, there was a day when I watched a man walk across a street. Cleve Fraser. He walked across that street to meet another man, a man with a gun. I had never seen anything like it before. It did things to me inside. There was a flurry of shooting. And after that was done it was Cleve Fraser who stood there, unhurt. And I was never so thankful for anything in my life. Right then I knew that I never wanted anything ever to harm Cleve Fraser. If that sounds silly to you, it is still the truth. So that is why I wanted to get this word to Cleve, so that he might be warned in time. Which makes me both traitor and fool, no doubt."

A little tremor touched Sherry's lips and she pulled them taut to hide it.

Leslie Cormack had courage herself and she admired it in others. She knew that she had just witnessed a rather splendid exhibition of this virtue. Her tone and manner softened.

"You are being very generous. Your uncle—he would not like—"

Sherry's small shoulders shrugged but held resolute. "Uncle Pardee's business ethics are his own, not mine. I had never paid much attention to his past operations, in Ruby Valley or on Bidwell Plains. I was not around either place very much, being East most of the time, visiting. But here I've been right from the first. I've overheard talk and I've seen things. Maybe I feel that Uncle Pardee could destroy himself if he's not turned back. But also I know somehow that the whole thing is wrong, and that Cleve Fraser must be warned."

"But you don't owe Cleve a thing."

"Maybe I do. More than anyone can realize. Like—like an understanding of values I'd never considered before. At any rate, he must be warned."

"He will be," promised Les Cormack. "Come with me!"

They rode at a fast lope, heading for Shield and Cross. They rode in silence, each with her thoughts and each strangely aware of a certain kinship because of their sex and mutual feeling. Coming in on Shield and Cross headquarters, Les Cormack finally spoke again.

"You must come in and tell Dad what you've told me about that Rafter X herd. He'll handle the rest."

They slowed to a jog, and then Sherry Dane pulled to a halt. "I'd rather not go in," she said. "I could open up to you, and you, being one of us fool women, could understand. But it would serve no point in my saying the same things to your father, who might wonder at my honesty. So it's better that I ride along now. This is probably good-by, Leslie Cormack. I shall be going East again before very long."

Les considered her soberly. "Knowing Cleve, I'm sure he'd want to thank you."

"Thanks," said Sherry Dane, very steadily, "would be all—and not enough. There, now you know everything. But you see, my dear, I've seen Cleve Fraser look at you. And a man like him looks at only one woman that way—ever. You are a very lucky person."

Small boot heels thumped equine ribs, and then Sherry

Dane was racing away. Her head was high and her shoulders straight and gallant.

11. *Summer Range*

CATTLE IN THE TIMBER. CATTLE SWARMING, MOVING leisurely, but ever higher, up the great flank of the Sentinels. Cattle in little groups and in long, ragged lines, working out in their own way the easier angles of the slope. Up gulches they traveled, where the forest mold lay deep and soft. And along ridge tops where the timber thinned and the sun had had its chance to work fully, so that plodding hoofs chopped up a dust that lifted and hung and winnowed through timber tops in a fine golden-amber haze. And as the sun climbed and pressed increasingly down, the baked, resinous breath of the forest laid its own peculiar savor in a man's throat.

Moving along in the drag of the herd, constantly drifting right and left to keep the inevitable stragglers moving, Cleve Fraser knew a stir of the old satisfaction which these drives up to summer range had always given him. He liked the timber, with its broken patterns of sunlight and shadow, and he liked its piny fragrance. He liked its cloistered serenity and the soft stir of the wind in its lofty crests and the air's increasingly thin purity as the climb lengthened.

Most of all he liked the goal of the movement, the high green meadows and parks where, even in midsummer, a man rose at dawn with frost crackling on his bed tarp. Days under a high, free sun that warmed without oppressing, and nights with the stars brilliant and close and a campfire giving off ruddy cheer and comfort, with all hands lounging in content within the circle of its light. Up there a man was a long way from a troubled world.

A sweating, hard-working horse came up from below and dropped in beside Fraser. Fraser turned to look at Sam Tepner, foreman of Shield and Cross.

"How is it, Sam?" asked Fraser in some surprise. "Has Alec Cormack decided to drift some of his herd up here after all?"

Tepner shook his head. "Not that pleasant and simple, Cleve. Rafter X has got that idea. About a thousand head, pointed for the Garden. Plenty of riders, plenty of guns. Alec figured you'd like to know."

The musing content which pleasant thoughts had built up wiped swiftly from Fraser's face, replaced by a ripple of harshness. "So Pardee Dane wants it rough, eh?"

"Would seem so," said Tepner. "Alec's sending the rest of the crew along soon as they get necessary gear together. He's also sent word to Art Wilcoxon and Dab Shurtleff. Aims to suggest they throw in with you and us on this thing as a common chore, figuring that it's all or nothing for all of us."

"How did Alec hear of this Rafter X herd?" Fraser rapped.

"Why, it seems that Les was out riding and she bumped into that pretty little niece of Dane's. And Dane's niece told Les."

"Sherry Dane!" exclaimed Fraser, dumfounded. "And she told Les?"

"That's right. Told Les to see that you were warned."

Fraser was silent for a long moment. "Why should she want to warn us of her uncle's plans?"

"Hell!" Sam Tepner shrugged. "How would I know? I never did waste time trying to figure out how a woman's mind works, because there never is any telling. Anyhow, Les is certain she got the truth. And it won't take too long to check up."

Soddy Joens was working the east flank of the herd and Fraser sought him out. "Take over, Soddy. Swing the cattle farther west. Take them into White Horse Glades. Enough grass and water there to hold over for two or three days if we have to."

Soddy's eyes sharpened. "Something's up. Thunder along the ridges, mebbe?"

"Maybe," said Fraser. "Let you know. Come on, Sam."

They swung directly east, putting their horses to it, and they rode fast and in silence. In time they came out on the crest of a ridge above the canyon where Red Bank Creek found its beginnings. Here they got their answer quickly. A long half mile below them thin dust haze was drifting up through the timber, and faint but definitely sounded the rumble of cattle, voicing bellowing complaint against driven movement.

"Why, now," said Sam Tepner, "I reckon there comes our trouble, Cleve. How high you figure they'll get by evening?"

"Not too far. Probably to the benches around Tamarack Springs. If I was bringing cattle up this way, that's where I'd head for. Mallory probably has it figured the same. Let's get out of here."

Heading back at a more leisurely pace, Fraser was locked in grim thoughts. Here, he knew, was showdown. Pardee Dane had played a trump card, thrown the issue right in his face and in that of every other resident cattleman along the range. If Dane got away with this, then he would try more. They could quit right now, or they could settle the issue once and for all, right here in these eternal hills.

Another thought that raked his mind back and forth was the fact of Sherry Dane's warning. What had prompted it? He thought of that evening in the kitchen of his own ranch house, of the miserable, disillusioned ending of it. And the judgment he had rendered there so savagely he took back now in large part. People were what they were, and no one could ever fully understand the depths of all the others. His mood grew somber and introspective as he rode.

Sam Tepner spoke just once. "Damn tough world at times, Cleve. A man works plenty for what he gets and then has to fight to hold it. Maybe that makes it worth more. I wouldn't know."

They found the Saber herd already at White Horse Glades. Happy Harte was setting up a cooking fire, while Danny Cope worked with the pack string, unloading food and bedding and other gear. Soddy Joens and Big Bob Scanlon were throwing up a rope corral for the small remuda. Fraser called them together and gave them the story.

There was a short silence. Then Soddy Joens said, "Hell of a way to start a pleasant summer. Aggravates me, this does. I'm liable to get real rough with some of them Rafter X jingos. Bump Grat Mallory right in the teeth, should the chance come my way."

Big Bob Scanlon looked at Soddy with a small grin. He knew what a wicked old wolf Soddy could be in a fight. "Toughest talk I ever heard you make, Soddy. You must have been feeding on raw meat."

They passed it off this way, idly joshing. But deep inside every one of them was deadly serious, knowing the odds and chances and accepting them fully.

Danny Cope was especially solemn as he went back to his chore, and observing this, Soddy Joens presently drifted over that way, keeping his tone mildly conversational when he spoke.

"Cleve Fraser would wade through hell barefooted for a friend, kid. Us that know him will follow him through the same place in a scrap. How about you?"

Danny looked squarely at the lean old puncher and saw that Soddy knew all he knew. Soddy wasn't tossing the rawhide about. He just knew full well what could lie ahead and was making sure there would be no weak links. Holding Soddy's glance, Danny said, "I'll be at Cleve's right hand, Soddy, no matter what comes."

Soddy's glance probed for a moment, and then he nodded, dropping a hand on Danny's shoulder. "Sure you will, kid," he murmured. "Sure you will."

Danny dug into his chore with furious energy, glad to have this moment to himself. He was all filled up inside. Soddy had given his stamp of approval and this, added to all Cleve Fraser had said and done for him, made him feel that now he really was one of Saber's tight, taut little crew. The harassing sense of guilt that had weighed so heavily was somehow much lighter now.

In the first dusk Art Wilcoxon and Dab Shurtleff rode in at the head of their men. With them was the balance of the Shield and Cross crew. Greeting was brief and matter-of-fact.

"Appreciate this, of course," Fraser told Wilcoxon and Shurtleff. "It's fight, you understand—and not over your range."

Art Wilcoxon shrugged. "In one way, no—but in another, yes. If Pardee Dane pushed you out of the picture, Cleve, why then he'd be sure to take a sight on the rest of us. We agreed with Alec Cormack that the smart thing to do is put all the chips on this hand. For if you win, we all win."

"That's it," grunted Dab Shurtleff. "Whole hog or none. In the Bunch Grass deal we all tried to play a lone hand and got our ears beat off. We play it different this trip, like we should have played it then. Rafter X is honin' for a row, so we'll give 'em one."

Immediately on arriving Dobie Roon had gone over to help Happy Harte at the fire and soon there was a meal ready. They ate it hunkered around the fire, a circle of grave-faced men, thoroughly dedicated to the idea of concerted effort in what lay ahead.

On a ridge point above the glades a thick-limbed figure crouched behind a down log and watched the camp below. Beede Helser was a crooked man and a ruthless one, but possessed of a certain shrewd cunning. And as he crouched there, Helser was putting two and two together and coming up with an answer that pleased him immensely.

He had bought several jags of rustled cattle from Danny Cope and Vance Ogden and wanted more. So earlier in this day he had ridden in to the Lockyear cabin with the idea of getting word to Cope and Ogden that he was ready for another deal. But the Lockyears had some news for Helser that didn't augur too well for the future. Vance Ogden, so the Lockyears had claimed, had been caught red-handed on another rustling job, and hung to a tall tree. They didn't know what had happened to Danny Cope, but they were very sure about Vance Ogden. All of which gave Beede Helser something to think about in several ways.

One thing was very certain. Rustled stock would be much harder come by from now on. He'd have to go after them himself, rather than sit back in comparative security and let others take the big risks. Again, before Vance Ogden had swung, had he talked? If so, how much? And Danny Cope—had he skipped the country, or was he trapped and in custody somewhere, and maybe talking?

In the event either Ogden or Cope had talked, and talked enough, then another thing was very certain. There was nothing but a risky future for Beede Helser on this side of the Sentinels. Helser didn't like uncertainty. He was a stolid man, liked things once planned to stay planned, once set to stay set. And now he didn't know. There was only one way to be sure, and that was to do some careful riding and find out some answers for himself.

So he had ridden, drifting west along the flank of the Sentinels. From a lofty point he had spent some time carefully studying the long roll of country below. He had picked up a long, persistent, though thin haze of dust lifting along the ridges leading up toward Tamarack Springs. And still farther west, barely discernible across the far distance, was another faint dust haze, working up into the Sentinels above Cleve Fraser's headquarters.

Cattle. Cattle in the timber. Two herds, both moving into the higher reaches of the mountains. There was only one answer, and Beede Helser got it. Saber cattle and Rafter X cattle, both driving for the same objective, the high meadow summer range in the Sentinels. Which pointed inevitably to another conclusion. Battle somewhere, between Saber and Rafter X, battle to a finish. But Helser wanted to be doubly sure, so he had circled and dropped to a lower level and then worked in cautiously from the side until close enough to identify positively that it was Rafter X working up toward Tamarack Springs.

After this Helser worked wide to the west to come finally upon this camp in White Horse Glades. He had reached this spot while the first Saber cattle were beginning to mass out into the glades and he had settled down to get all the rest of the picture that he could.

He had seen the camp being set up, and he saw Cleve Fraser and Sam Tepner come riding in from the east, saw Fraser call his men about him and talk to them. Now, later, he'd seen Wilcoxon and Shurtleff ride in with their own and the Shield and Cross crew. Beede Helser put all these items together and came up with the only answer: War across the Sentinels.

Now Helser settled back on his heels, a brute bulk of

a man, his broad, heavy face reflecting a satisfaction all his own. He measured his own interests in this thing and what he could profit from it. And the profit ran big, if he handled things right.

If only Fraser and his Saber crew were down there with the cattle, then conflict with Rafter X, though inevitable, would not have been an immediate prospect. Days, maybe weeks, before the showdown would come. But Fraser and his Saber crew weren't alone. They had three other outfits siding them which, as Beede Helser figured it, meant immediate action.

He wondered if Grat Mallory knew about this massing of forces? If Mallory didn't, and was caught with a surprise attack, Rafter X might very well be smashed, quickly and finally. Which Helser didn't want to happen, for there would be no profit for himself in such a finish. What Helser wanted was a battle that would cut up and ruin both groups. That would give him plenty of room to work in, and the profits would be—well—!

Beede Helser drew a deep breath, took another look at the camp below, then backed carefully away from his lookout, got his horse, and cut east through the dark timber. An hour and a half later he was facing Grat Mallory across one of the campfires now burning at Tamarack Springs.

"Helser," said Mallory, "you're a damned cow thief. I know it and you know it. This way and that I've heard plenty about you. You ought to be hung!"

Beede Helser stood, spreadlegged, unabashed, a hard grin on his face. "Old saying about the pot calling the kettle black, Mallory," he retorted boldly. "But we won't go into that. The big point is what I've just told you. Fraser's got three outfits beside his own over at White Horse Glades. Do I have to write it in a book to show you what that means?"

"No," growled Mallory, "you don't. But you could be lying."

"I could be but I'm not. And you know that, because there'd be no point in it."

Mallory considered this, scowling. "You're not telling me this out of the goodness of your heart, Helser. You see profit in it somewhere for yourself."

"That's right, I do." Helser's hard grin was still working. "I never work for fun. You bust Fraser and the rest of that crowd and I'll make out all right."

Mallory understood then. "And if Fraser managed to bust Rafter X, then you'd still make out all right—on Rafter X cattle, is that it?"

"The fight," said Helser, "is between you and Fraser. I'm playing along with what I figure is the strong side. There'll be plenty of Saber cattle running loose when this is over. I'll take my pick."

"I could," reminded Mallory, "give one yell and you'd never leave this camp alive."

Beede Helser's eyes glinted, but his grin stayed on, jeering. "Nice reward that would be for me bringing you this word. Yet I thought of such a possibility. You give that yell, Mallory, and it'll be your last. I don't always work alone, you know. Maybe somebody's got you in the sights of a Winchester right now."

Grat Mallory's head jerked up and his head swung warily as his glance touched the surrounding blackness of the timber. Helser went on, reminding, "You're a fat target in this firelight."

"All right," rapped Mallory. "You've told me. Now get out! You'll still live to hang."

"A possibility every man has to face," mocked Helser, backing away into the shadows.

Grat Mallory sat for some time by the fire. He knew that the hand had been dealt, and that he had to play the cards he held. He mused over what Beede Helser had told him and, though the man was a thoroughly unsavory scoundrel, he knew Helser had told him the truth. Because, as Helser had frankly admitted, it served his interests in this case to do so. Those massed outfits over with the Saber herd could mean only one thing—the thing which Cleve Fraser had promised Pardee Dane. Trouble! Trouble if Dane started to move Rafter X cattle into the Sentinels.

Considering all the angles with an objective shrewdness, Mallory came to the same logical answer as Beede Helser. Cleve Fraser wouldn't be taking Wilcoxon and Shurtleff and their outfits, along with Shield and Cross, into the mountains just to guard Saber cattle, or to push them on the drive into the mountains. That didn't make sense. The only reason for the massed outfits was that Fraser meant to attack, to carry this fight right to Rafter X. The attack, when it came, would be an attempted surprise, and probably at the earliest opportunity. Which could very well mean this night, or early tomorrow morning.

The more Grat Mallory turned this thing over in his mind the more certain he became that he had the right answers. But, and now Mallory's eyes took on a hard glitter, if that attempted surprise should boomerang—if, instead of Fraser finding a Rafter X outfit relaxed and unawares he found one set and waiting for him, a force ready and able to cut him and his followers to pieces, why then wouldn't the big question over the whole range be answered?

Handled right, in one roaring showdown, not only Saber, but Shield and Cross, Running W, and Split Circle, all would be broken and scattered, and then Rafter X could take over all they wanted and at their leisure. Pardee Dane would have his new range empire and he, Grat Mallory, would be riding high and pretty. Yes, sir! A lot of things could be evened up, if he played this one right.

Grat Mallory paused to play with one more thought— the satisfaction that would be his when he got Cleve Fraser over the sights of a gun. And no blame could be pointed at Rafter X. Rafter X would only be protecting itself. The onus would be on Fraser and those riding with him. They would start the battle, but Rafter X would finish it!

Mallory stood up, called in Chess Breshear and Loop Scarlett, and began laying out plans.

Beede Helser, drifting back through the night and riding high, came in above White Horse Glades again just in time to see a dark mass of riders move out and head east, toward Tamarack Springs.

One man alone remained with the Saber herd, squatting by the fire. Danny Cope.

Beede Helser laughed softly. His luck was turning out

good this night. For this setup couldn't be better. Cope was down there, and he knew how to handle Cope. The significance of Danny Cope being one of Fraser's crew was a little thick for Helser to figure out, but he didn't worry any about that. He still knew he could handle Cope without any trouble.

For a long time after the others had ridden off Danny Cope sat by the fire. His first reaction when Cleve Fraser had told him he'd have to stay with the cattle and not go along to take part in the attack on Rafter X had left Danny deep sunk in dejection. For Danny had wanted mightily to be in on that thing, if for no other reason than to drive out the skepticism he'd seen in Dab Shurtleff's eyes and in the eyes of several other Split Circle and Running W and Shield and Cross riders.

Danny wanted to show these men that he wasn't afraid to ride into the toughest kind of a spot, that he was now as true and good a man as any of them, that this was the kind of man he'd always meant to be and finally was.

Not that Danny was anxious to die, smashed down by wild lead in a furious dawn battle. Danny was never so anxious to live. For now the trail was straight and there was Teresa and all the future of a fine, great world. But Danny knew that someway, somehow, he had to prove, once and for all, beyond any doubt of others or within himself, that he was really a man among men. And then Cleve Fraser had told him he was to stay with the cattle.

Cleve had seen the first eagerness in Danny's eyes and then saw it fade and die out when he gave Danny the order. With that rare understanding that only a truly generous man could possess, Fraser had dropped an arm around Danny's young shoulders.

"Kid," he said quietly, "somebody has got to stay with the herd. Those cows out there represent most of what I, and my father before me, have managed to chew out of this tough old world. I wouldn't trust them with every man."

And that did it, of course. That tied Danny up inside again, made his throat thick and his eyes queerly blurred. For not so long ago this man, Cleve Fraser, had caught him red-handed, caught him rustling. And this was Cleve's way of telling him, once and for all, that those mistaken days were forgotten history, a mistake that was dead and buried and that here was offered a complete trust. So now Danny didn't feel bad any more. As long as Cleve Fraser believed in him, and Teresa did, well, the rest didn't matter.

Danny smoked out another cigarette by the fire, then went and got his horse and rode a slow and careful circle about the glades, holding the cattle well in there, where they were already beginning to bed down. When Danny got back to the fire it was beginning to gutter toward coals and he did not try to build it up again. He spun another cigarette and hunkered down, set for an all-night watch. And it was now that a voice sounded behind him.

"Cope, this is the chance you and me been waiting for all our lives!"

For a long moment Danny Cope did not stir. That voice—he remembered it. How well he remembered it! He turned his head and said, "Hello, Helser. What brings you way over here?"

Beede Helser moved up beside Danny with a heavy-legged, rolling step. He made a thick, bull-shouldered figure in the fire's thinning light. A sly and chilling grin pulled at his heavy lips.

"Just drifting around, having a look at things. Mighty interesting ride. Lot of white-faces bunched over around Tamarack Springs and another fat herd here. When the big fellows get to warring among themselves, that's when the little fellow comes into his own. Strikes me a couple of enterprising men could do right well by themselves tonight. Stir up that fire and get busy. I'm hungry."

Helser's first words had been smooth, almost careless. His last carried a rough, harsh snap.

Danny Cope didn't argue. He freshened the fire, cooked coffee and bacon from the grub packs. Beede Helser watched him with unwinking intentness. A little chill began working up Danny's spine. Helser's first words had shown which way this man's mind was working, and Danny knew that now he had a part to play and he set about playing it. He made his moves about the fire as casual and offhand as he could.

"Heard about Ogden getting strung," went on Helser. "Didn't surprise me much. That hombre wasn't right. Weak stuff underneath. Don't tell me he was workin' alone?"

"No, he wasn't," said Danny. "I was along, but I was lucky. I got clear without being seen." Danny knew he had to lie and lie convincingly. "It was close with me—damned close. Where's Frank and Hardy?"

Helser twitched a careless shoulder. "They got stubborn and too big for their britches. Weren't satisfied with their share of the profits. Set up to argue about it. Mistake on their part. For I got no patience with stubborn people."

The chill along Danny's spine deepened. Here was both statement and threat. Helser didn't have to elaborate for Danny to understand. Frank and Hardy, who'd been Helser's companions at the time of that last deal on rustled cattle, were dead. And Helser had killed them in some argument over the proceeds. Danny built another smoke, concentrating so that his hands worked without tremor. He thought of the last time he'd seen Frank and Hardy, over at the Lockyear cabin. Rough and conscienceless scoundrels maybe, but loyal enough to Helser, and trusting him. But they were dead now. And Helser had killed them. . . .

"You're ridin' guard over Saber cattle," said Helser. "That I can't figure—you workin' for Fraser. What's the idea—you gettin' religion?" Helser's glance bored at Danny.

Danny shrugged with convincing carelessness. "I told you it was awful close for me the other day—too close. And after what happened to Ogden I figured I'd better ride for wages again until things quieted down. Fraser was looking for an extra hand, so I took on with him."

Hunkered down across the fire, Helser watched Danny fork sputtering bacon over and over in the pan, sniffed its keen fragrance and that of bubbling coffee with hungry intentness. When the food was ready he gulped his coffee greedily and ate with a rough and hungry haste.

"No man ever got rich ridin' for wages, Cope," he mumbled. "Now here's our chance to make a real stake. I been around here watchin' since this herd first hit these glades. I saw Fraser and the rest ride out. I know where they're going and I know what they figure to do when they get there. Even if they're lucky it could be noon or even later tomorrow before any of them get back here. Maybe they won't be that lucky. Maybe, by the time the smoke clears away, this herd won't even have an owner any more. See what I'm driving at?"

Danny Cope saw, all right, and he could see what else was coming. He touched his lips with the tip of his tongue, eyes fixed on the fire. He watched a thin filament of flame lick in and out of a glowing coal. Each time the flame showed weaker and thinner, and presently it did not show at all any more. And the coal, so dying, began to turn gray. That was the way, Danny thought, that life could run out of a man.

"You and me," said Beede Helser, "we'll take as big a chunk of this herd as we can manage and drive all night. Timber thins fast up above. Come daylight we'll have a real start. I figure we can be over the crest of the mountains before Fraser and his crowd, even if they're lucky, can get back here. It'll take them more time to get things sorted out and hit our trail, even if they ain't too shot up to care. Yeah, Cope, here's our chance to make a real stake."

Danny fenced for time, desperate inside, casual outside. "There's snow higher up. Enough to make it tough getting past the crest. You're forgetting that, Helser."

"Hell I am! Sure there's some snow, but not too much

to block all the high passes. I tell you I know these mountains. We can do it. We can get across."

A grayness came down over Danny's mind. There's no way out of this but him or me, he thought. And I'm not as fast as he is. I got no chance of getting there first without a break of some kind. And he's going to force it, yes or no! He's asking me to sell out Cleve Fraser, the whitest man who ever walked. He's asking me to sell out Teresa and her folks. He's asking me to sell out myself, after I got my feet on the good trail. He'd use me and then kill me, just as he did Frank and Hardy. He's a two-legged wolf and he's expecting me to be a dog of the lowest water. So ran Danny's thoughts.

Beede Helser was staring at Danny as though, with his little, glinting eyes, he would peer into the deepest corner of Danny's mind and see what was in there. Danny steeled his will to hold the pressure back. And all the time a part of his brain was shouting at him that he had to find a break—a break of some kind. . . .

Helser drained the last of his coffee, began building another cigarette, and now a new, hard note of deadliness came into his voice. "I told you I didn't cotton to stubborn people, Cope. I'm going to take a fat chunk of this herd and drive. I'm going to do it even if I have to do it alone. And if I do go it alone you can bet I ain't leaving a witness behind in shape to talk—ever. Make up your mind, Cope!"

Helser's heavy teeth came together with a click on this last word. Then he licked his cigarette into shape, brought out a match, snapped it alight, and lifted it in cupped hands to his cigarette. And right then Danny made up his mind! Here was the break—the break he'd been looking and praying for.

Danny, rocking on his heels, tipped over, falling on his left side, and his right hand slashed at his gun. He felt the hard, cold butt of it full and solid in his hand and at the pull it came smoothly from the holster. Danny had the gun free and he pushed it toward that thick and menacing figure beyond the fire.

A gusty curse erupted from Beede Helser. Had he dived right across the fire at Danny Cope, it might have done him some good. But, a gunman, he thought only in terms of guns. So he lunged partially up, the lighted match dropping in a brief curve from his fingers, his hands pushing down, fast—very fast!

Danny Cope's gun drove back in pounding recoil against the tension of his wrist, once and then again. Report swelled up and slammed back and forth across the glades. Beede Helser lurched and swayed but stayed up there. Danny shot a third time. Helser coughed thickly, spun in a slow half circle, and fell.

Danny got to his feet, staring across the glades. The crashing echoes had brought a number of the bedded cattle to their feet and their gusty snorts of alarm were a hard breathing across the night. But they didn't run, and the rising stir held for a moment, then began to still and settle back again.

Danny slowly circled the fire. A cold and queasy sickness rumpled his stomach. Part of it was the raw, wicked tension running out of him. The rest was from the knowledge that this was the first time his gun had ever done a thing like this. He went over to a pack, got a blanket and spread it over Beede Helser.

Danny was dripping with sweat. It was even in his eyes, salt and stinging. He cleared it away with a scrubbing sleeve and then stood for a long time, dragging deep of the night air. There was a tremor in his knees and the muscles of his legs felt rubbery. Gunsmoke's acridness hovered for a time, then went away on the wings of a little night breeze that came slipping through the timber.

Finally Danny began to steady down and his thoughts to clear. The queer, shaking weakness went out of his legs and the queasiness in his stomach left. He realized that here had been a time when fate had thrown all the proof of his past and his future into a single roll of the dice. He'd had a single choice to make and he'd made it. He'd ridden along with fate, put it all on a single toss. A gamble he'd never want to take again, but out of this one he'd come whole and big. A true man who would, from now on, always be true.

12. Long Tally

ON THE DARK SLOPE OF THE SENTINELS, WELL ABOVE Tamarack Springs, Cleve Fraser waited out the slow run of the night's hours. In the stillness about him other men did the same. Some were dozing, some even sleeping soundly, the unimaginative ones. Others, like Fraser, were taking the wait wide-eyed and stoic.

They had laid their plans for this thing before leaving White Horse Glades. They would hit Grat Mallory and his Rafter X crew in the first breaking gray of dawn, coming down upon them from above with all the weight they could muster. It was a plan that had met with complete approval all around.

"Best time of day to pull a surprise," Soddy Joens had said. "Just at dawn. The Injuns knew that."

After reaching this position, Soddy had come forth with another suggestion which had also been accepted. Just before dawn Art Wilcoxon would take a couple of men and work around to the east side of Tamarack, while Dab Shurtleff would do the same on the west side.

"A feller trying to concentrate on what's lookin' him dead in the eye can sure be mighty upset and disturbed by somebody chuckin' rocks at him from the side," summed up Soddy. " 'Specially when he ain't expectin' it."

But the major part of the crews, with Fraser leading, would come down from above in that fast, hard rush, calculated to throw the Rafter X herd into wild stampede downhill. Once they got that herd started, nothing could stop it short of the bottom.

It was, mused Fraser, easy enough to lay out such a plan. But it wouldn't be so simple to put into effect. It would be wild riot and there would be dead men to face the next day's sun with sightless eyes. It was something no sane and balanced man wanted, but it was something which had to be done. If it were not, then the days of all else but Rafter X interests across the range would be numbered.

Considering these things in the silence of his thoughts, Cleve Fraser knew a thin and bitter rage toward the guiding minds behind the Rafter X maneuvering. Toward Pardee Dane, that cold-eyed, cold-minded man who, although holding so much, was still reaching and grabbing for more. Playing this thing like a game of chess, with the lives of other men as pawns and the power of his wealth and influence as his queen. Men like Pardee Dane had laid a pattern of graves all across the West and neither cared nor knew remorse.

Then there was Grat Mallory, with his smooth, dark face, his shadowed eyes, and his faint, sly smile. A malignant man who touched others and turned them bad. As he had done with Vance Ogden. And so Vance was dead, dying a savage and dishonored death that could leave its scar on others for a lifetime.

Thought of Mallory made Fraser stir restlessly. That man had never fooled him, not from the first. Instinct had set him against Mallory from the first time they met. This same instinct had told Fraser that someday, somewhere, he and Mallory were fated to settle all things between them in one final roaring showdown. Maybe this dawn they were waiting for would be the start of that day. Maybe . . . !

Fraser shook himself. There were always a thousand maybes. . . .

Later, Fraser thought he must have dozed some of the dragging time away, for now there was a stir at his elbow which was Soddy Joens coming up silent as a ghost.

"Time to get movin', Cleve," murmured Soddy. "First light will be showing in another half-hour. Best stir up Wilcoxon and Shurtleff and send them on their way.

And the rest of us should move in closer before we bust loose on the big run."

Fraser got to his feet, stretched the cramp from his muscles, tipped his face to the dark's chill, moist breath. They understood each other, he and Soddy did. Soddy, grizzled and wise and liking the pose of an acid pessimism to cover a really keen appreciation of the savor of life. Soddy, who was faithful and as gentle or as tough as the occasion required. Soddy had been riding for Saber ever since Fraser was a long-legged stripling and, though Fraser had long since reached man's full estate, with confidence in his own decisions, he liked to have the balance of Soddy's opinion to back up his own.

"What do you think, Soddy?"

"We've done our thinkin'," answered Soddy. "We've figured ourselves some answers, and we hope the right ones. So now the hand is dealt and there's nothin' to do but play it the best way we can."

They went over and stirred up Wilcoxon and Shurtleff, who called in their respective men. Fraser walked with Wilcoxon and Shurtleff to their horses, a hand on either man's shoulder.

"Win, lose, or draw," he said slowly, "we've gained something out of this."

They knew what he meant. A common cause had drawn them closer together than ever before in their lives. If they came out of this whole, then they would have achieved that rare kind of friendship that made any man's life more rich and satisfying.

"No draw, no lose," growled Dab Shurtleff. "We'll win, Cleve."

And Art Wilcoxon added, "Take care of yourself, fellah. You'll be the one spittin' right in their eye."

Wilcoxon and Shurtleff and their men rode off, circling right and left, wary and careful in the dark. When they were fifteen minutes gone, Fraser began moving down slope with his own force.

In the east the horizon line was no longer black, but brushed with a chill and growing grayness. The stars had lost their luster, seemed to be slipping away into some vast and hiding distance. A stir of life was beginning to tumble up across the world, a stir that was sensed rather than felt or heard or seen. The world was waking and dawn was moving in.

They quickened their pace, reaching the crest of the sharp down pitch which led into the benchland where lay Tamarack Springs. A dawn breeze, sweeping up the mountain flank, carried to them the sound and smell of a cattle herd beginning to stir to a new day. The bawl of a critter carried up, a lonely sound across the dawn's great waking.

"We'd best get at it," said Soddy Joens quietly. "When cow critters begin to stir, men start rollin' out of their blankets."

Cleve Fraser stood high in his stirrups. He had the feeling of a man about to take a leap into black depths, the extent of which was surmised and hopefully calculated but not truly known. Here was a move which, once committed to, could not be recalled. It had to be carried all the way. It was the trail of no return.

He filled his lungs and let go with a hard, shrill yell. His spurs dug in, and in one long lunge his dun horse was over the crest and racing down into the shadows. Behind him came the others. Taking their cue from him, they sent a high, wild crying down across the startled world.

There was a thin barrier of scattered jack pines, and through this Fraser's big dun horse broke with a powerful plunging, hurtling into the clear beyond. On one side of Fraser rode Soddy Joens, on the other Dobie Roon, of Wilcoxon's outfit. No man ever rode into battle flanked by two stronger supports than these rawhide tough old punchers.

It had been Fraser's thought that once beyond the jack pines they would probably strike the upper fringe of the Rafter X herd. But this was not so; no cattle were here. Nothing was here but emptiness. Forty—sixty—seventy-five yards below the jack pines they raced and still no cattle. A sudden chill knotted Fraser's stomach. Something was wrong here. Something . . . !

A yell whipped out from dawn's tricky shadows ahead, a yell that was immediately lost in a running line of winking gun flame and flat, bellowing reports. Belting echoes clubbed at a man with a peculiar power all their own.

On Fraser's left a bullet told with an ominous crunch and grim old Dobie Roon, who wielded a cook's skillet in peace but a use worn gun in war, humped far over his saddle horn for two more jumps of his horse, then piled headlong down to the dark earth and the everlasting shadows.

Something fanned Fraser's face with a waspish hiss, and farther along a horse screamed wildly, reared, and collapsed in a tangle of thrashing hoofs, throwing its rider loose and rolling.

It was Soddy Joens who got the full significance of this thing first and voiced it with a long shout. "Back! Get back into the jack pines! We've rode into something! Back!"

Fraser set the dun up hard, the big horse sliding and rearing as it fought to brake against the slope and make the turn. There was a smashing blow, and Fraser thought the dun must be hit until he punched a hand down against his saddle horn to brace himself against the dun's frantic scrambling. Under his hand the saddle horn was a shattered mess of bullet-torn leather and rawhide.

The dun, finally fully around, wild with the excitement of this thing, drove powerfully back up slope into the jack pines. On his head Fraser's hat shifted slightly. Maybe the whip of a branch, maybe the whip of something far more deadly. On either hand horses were crashing through the cover and men were cursing in a thin and scalding fury. Fraser yelled, "Soddy!"

"Right here," answered Soddy, close by. "Cleve, they knew we were coming. They were waiting for us!"

Fraser yelled again. "Out of your saddles, everybody! Get close to the ground and give it back to them!"

His heels dug into the soft mold of the slope and he dragged his rifle from the scabbard under his stirrup leather. Then he drove down to the thicket's edge. The clamor of guns from below was one long, crashing roll. Lead ripped steadily into the jack pines, showering down shredded debris. Bullets told solidly against firmer wood and one, glancing off something, wailed away in a ricochet's quick rising then equally quick-fading whine. A horse, bullet stung but not disabled, raced crazily off through the tangle, and a man cried bitterly, "Who got the surprise? Us—not them!"

"Steady!" answered Soddy Joens, bleakly harsh. "This pot's just opened. Get low and give back some of what they're sendin'."

Hunched on one knee at the edge of the jack pines, Cleve Fraser ran through every shell in his rifle, holding under those winking gun flashes below. He threw each bullet as he would a muscular blow, swinging the rifle's lever swiftly, knowing a fierce satisfaction in the thump of recoil against his shoulder. When the rifle clicked empty and he began shoving fresh shells into the loading gate, then Soddy Joens, but a few feet away, set another rifle to snarling. Fraser, watching, saw some of the gun flashes below waver raggedly. Soddy knew this sort of business, could be wicked at it.

The first confusion over, fire from the jack pines quickened and grew. And Soddy Joens, his gun now empty, spoke almost calmly as he reloaded.

"This is a lot better. That gang below made one big mistake. They opened up too soon. If they'd waited until we got closer they'd have cut us to rags before we could get back to this cover. As it is, we've got the elevation on them and things are gettin' a mite uncomfortable down below. You all right, Cleve?"

"All right," rapped Fraser harshly. "But I've led the boys into something. If I hadn't been so damn sure—!"

"Nothin's sure—ever," soothed Soddy. "I tell you, they're gettin' anxious down below. And wait until

Wilcoxon and Shurtleff buy in!"

It was at this moment that Wilcoxon and Shurtleff began to buy in. From both right and left added guns sent more echoes rocketing. The effect was almost immediate. The raggedness of the Rafter X line of fire grew more pronounced, and then Grat Mallory's voice lifted in a shrill and angry yell.

"Breshear right—Scarlett left! Watch those flanks!"

"Ha!" exulted Soddy Joens. "The pinch is on. Somethin' is goin' to give down below."

For long minutes the battle ran its way. The gunfire was in uneven gusts, fading almost out one moment, then lifting to a high and angry peak of sound. Dawn light grew and brought discernible substance out of what had been illusory and shrouding shadow. Fraser, watching, searching with more care for targets, now that the first impotent surge of anger had burned out, caught a skulking figure in movement on the bench below and shot for the first time with certainty. He saw the figure stumble and fall.

"Damn!" said Soddy Joens evenly. "You shot that one right out from under my sights. But this won't do. We got to put more pressure on them. It's risky, but I think we ought to ride in now."

From below a yell of panic drifted up. "Our horses! They've scattered our horses!"

Soddy Joens jumped to his feet. "Hear that? Wilcoxon or Shurtleff played it smart. They've put that crowd afoot. Here's our break! Up and at 'em!"

Fraser yelled, "We're going down, boys! Into your saddles! We're going in!"

Fraser located the dun, swung up, and went lashing out of the tangle. On either hand men burst out with him, heading down across the benchland at a wild run. Every man understood the advantage that had fallen to them. Rafter X was afoot, and only a saddle man could fully understand another saddle man's dismay over such a prospect.

Speeding hoofs closed distances fast. Fraser was surprised how light it had suddenly become. Dawn mounted swiftly toward day once it started. He saw men in the big, scattered timber across the bench. They were on foot, all of them, dodging from tree to tree. He saw one of these figures, racing to the left, stop in midstride, as though hitting an invisible wall. The man turned completely around, took two steps back the way he'd come, then fell on his face. Those flanking guns of Wilcoxon's and Shurtleff's were a deadly business.

Another man appeared suddenly from behind the massive bole of a towering ponderosa pine, gun stabbing flame that now was pale in growing day. And then the horse of Concho Payne, a Shield and Cross rider, was charging about with an empty saddle. The man who had fired the fatal shot ran out, tried to catch the horse as it whirled by. He got hold of a flying rein and began fighting the animal to a stop. But before he could get close enough to control the animal and win to the empty saddle, it was Sam Tepner who hurtled in and gunned the fellow into the ground from ten feet distance.

Resistance was something a man could sense as well as feel, both the rising strength of it and its lessening and breaking up. Cleve Fraser could sense that breaking up now. Several reasons for it entered. Grat Mallory's men knew no real allegiance beyond the limit of their wages, while the men who now drove at them so furiously were men who had made this range, who had spent their lifetimes here, who had dug their roots deep and built for the long run of their future. It was their land, and this made a difference.

For another thing, that flanking fire had been wicked and wholly unexpected. Mallory had guessed correctly the main attack from above and had been set for it. But he had not considered who might strike at his flanks. He could have held that frontal attack and broken it. But the flanking fire had raked his forces into near panic. And, finally, the Rafter X remuda had been broken and scattered, putting riding men afoot, a position they never had had and never would like.

The first break in a dyke was ever only a trickle. But the trickle could quickly become a flood. It was that way now. Fraser and his men slashed clear across the bench without being stopped and now came up against the herd that Mallory had held at the edge of the main-slope breakoff.

Soddy Joens, pounding up beside Fraser, yelled, "No better time to start 'em runnin' than now, Cleve. This can clean the slate!"

Cattle—white-faced cattle—the slope was packed and crawling with them, astir and uneasy from the wild madness above them. Fraser and Soddy and Sam Tepner and Happy Harte piled into them, with other riders striking right and left.

Guns slammed lead and flame into the ground before

bulging, terrified bovine eyes. Yells rocketed up, riata ends whirled and thudded. The cattle began to pack and drift, driving in tighter and tighter, shoving, lunging, bellowing, trampling. A living wall against which the pressure built and piled. The herd became a great, shaking mass, a gathering force that must soon explode in some direction. That direction was downward.

It was the core of the herd that began it. It took on power, a driving wedge that split the center. It took on speed, and its voice was a hoarse and bellowing thunder, while the solid mountainside seemed to shake under the roll of hoofs. Faster drove the wedge, driving through to become an avalanche, pouring down the vast slope.

It seemed to leave a vacuum behind it that sucked in the east and west flanks and fringes of the herd, sucked them in and pulled them along. It rolled and pounded on into the mists of the lower reaches, leaving behind a long and fading rumble and the heavy odors of animal frenzy and heat.

Fraser reined in, sent out his reaching yell. "That does it! Hold up—hold up!"

They came spurring in from either side, grim but jubilant. "Quick delivery of a thousand head of his best right back into Pardee Dane's lap!" exulted Soddy Joens. "Let him chaw on that!"

"Just part of the chore," reminded Sam Tepner harshly. "A fight still on our hands."

They rode back and across the bench. Some guns were still belting the echoes around, out on the flanks. "Split up," ordered Fraser. "Half that way, half this."

He led the way east, glimpsed a couple of skulking

figures. "Watch yourselves!" he yelled. "Lay off any more gun work and you won't be hurt!"

The pair of Rafter X men stepped warily into the clear, hands spread and half lifted, wanting no further part of this thing.

"Mallory?" rapped Fraser. "Where is he?"

"Don't know," growled one, "and don't give a damn! I'm sick of this mess. I'll punch cattle for forty and found, but my skin comes higher than that."

To the west all shooting had suddenly stopped, but over to the east flank guns were still pounding. Drawing Soddy Joens with him, Fraser spurred that way. Here a long-past storm had left a scattered tangle of blowdown timber and three figures were skulking through it, shooting back at targets neither Fraser nor Soddy could see.

One of the three figures rose to full height to draw sight on something. A rifle whanged thinly, and the figure melted down. Then Dab Shurtleff's heavy yell of triumph sounded. The other two skulkers came scrambling and dodging back toward Fraser and Soddy, not aware of them until they were within a short thirty yards. And these two were Chess Breshear and Grat Mallory!

"All right!" rapped Fraser. "You better call it quits!"

They came around, both of them, a trapped wildness in them. Then it was Chess Breshear who threw a shot with the speed of a striking snake. Fraser, his left hand high, reining the dun, felt fire and shock strike his left forearm, jerking it around and spinning the dun that way before the reins fell from nerveless fingers, and it was only this swift turn of the dun that pulled its rider clean away from the bullet Grat Mallory threw on the very heels of Breshear's shot.

Fraser drove a knee into the dun's shoulder to bring it back, facing the blowdown. He heard Soddy Joens shoot once—twice! He saw Chess Breshear go backward over a down log, saw his booted feet swing high then settle limply across the log. And he saw Grat Mallory, hung with indecision for one vital second, not knowing whether to try for Fraser again or for Soddy Joens.

Grat Mallory! There was no smooth and mocking slyness about him now. His dark face was convulsed, cross pulled with a thwarted madness. No mask here, no slippery elusiveness. Just the man's full measure of malignancy broken loose, hungry to strike and kill. Because here was the final hand, and the realization was upon Mallory that he hadn't held enough cards, after all, while those he had held he'd played badly.

Fraser's belt gun was heavy in his right hand, and now he bleakly dropped it into line and drove a single shot past the dun's nervous and weaving head.

Grat Mallory staggered and began to shrink down. His face was suddenly all drained skin and bony angles. Then the tautness ran out of him, his head rolled, and he fell at the edge of the blowdown, face to the patient earth.

Fraser's shot seemed to put a period to everything. Now there was no more shooting, and the silence which settled in seemed to hold the quality of thunder itself, so swift and abrupt was the change. But right after this came the thin, echoing clamor of men's voices, and Fraser heard Dab Shurtleff's weighty shout, calling to someone.

Soddy Joens pushed in beside Fraser, voice tight with concern. "Breshear got you somewhere, boy. How bad?"

Fraser looked at his left arm. The sleeve of his denim jumper was all soggy with blood between elbow and wrist and his nerveless hand was slimy with dripping crimson. He put away his gun and stepped from the saddle. Soddy dropped down beside him, helped him out of his jumper, made swift examination of the wound, and clucked with swift relief.

"Feels like so much lead," gritted Fraser, his lips pulled thin.

"The bone ain't smashed," Soddy said. "Slug skidded right along it, numbing it. It'll feel like something one hell of a lot different than lead before long, and you'll know when and how much. Steady, now, while I tie it up."

Now the benchland was all astir with riders moving in from all sides, and there were several figures on foot being rounded up and bunched. Dab Shurtleff and Art Wilcoxon came spurring in.

"Picked yourself up something, eh, Cleve?" growled Shurtleff. "Not too bad?"

"No," Fraser told him. "But I'm afraid some of our boys weren't as lucky."

"That I know," said Shurtleff harshly. "Skip Kent for one. He was right alongside of me when he got it. Two or three of the opposition made it pretty tough out on my side for a time. Last I saw of them they were ducking through this blowdown. I figure I got one of them. Mallory—you seen anything of him?"

Soddy Joens jerked his head. "Take a look, Dab."

Shurtleff twisted in his saddle, stared for a moment. Then he looked at Fraser. "You?"

Fraser nodded. "Breshear's yonder, past that log. Soddy handled him. There's another further out."

Soddy said, "I'll take a see."

Coming back, Soddy said simply, "Ace Scarlett. They were the tough three, Scarlett, Breshear, and Mallory. You stampede those horses, Dab?"

"Not me. Musta been Wilcoxon who did that. Damn smart move, Art."

Art Wilcoxon, grave and slender and straight, shrugged. "Seemed like a pretty good idea at the time. Cleve, Rafter X knew we were coming in."

"They knew," agreed Fraser. "How they learned, I don't know. But they knew. It was only that they made a bigger mistake than I did that saved our hides. They opened up on us too soon. They'd have shot us to rags if they'd let us get in closer before starting the smoke. As it is," he ended wearily, "we've paid our price."

They found out how stem a price when they began to ride around and call a tally. They found Dobie Roon, Concho Payne, and Skip Kent crumpled and still. Sam Tepner had a shallow groove along his ribs and Nate Lyons was stumbling around, still groggy from a savage fall when his horse had been shot out from under him.

Besides Mallory and Breshear and Scarlett there were two other Rafter X riders done for, while a third was in serious shape from a chest wound. So ran the grim tally.

Fraser looked over the Rafter X men who had been

206

rounded up and realized once more that Art Wilcoxon had pulled the shrewdest and most deciding stroke of the whole affair when he stampeded the Rafter X remuda. Being put afoot, Fraser mused, did something to a saddle man. It cut his stature and confidence in half. And these men, brought in from the outside, had never understood the full picture of this fight and what it meant to either side.

"I don't know what you men feel you owe Pardee Dane," Fraser told them harshly, "or how much you want to give him in return for what he gives you. But if you think it's worth it, you can stick around this country and try your luck again. Only next time it'll be twice as rough as it was today. Your choice. You'll leave all your guns here and start walking. If your feet hold out, you'll make it to Red Bank Creek headquarters. Get going!"

13. The Greater Strength

IN HIS OFFICE AT THE RAFTER X HEADQUARTERS ON RED Bank Creek Pardee Dane, for the first time in his life, knew the feeling of being trapped and helpless. This feeling was all the more unnerving and disconcerting because it was here, right in his own office, on his own property that it held him. He was undergoing a grim fight to keep the feeling hidden as he faced three grim-faced men across the room's narrow width: Cleve Fraser, Art Wilcoxon, and Dab Shurtleff.

Pardee Dane was remembering the last time he had faced these same three men in this same room. Not so very long ago when that meeting had taken place, either.

At that time they had laid some cards on the table, bluntly worded, starkly menacing cards. But they hadn't seemed cards of much account at that time, for then he, Pardee Dane, was riding the peak of his power, and his plans were working out in a satisfying sequence, and he felt secure and beyond any chance of defeat or failure.

Pardee Dane had long ago conceived a plan, a plan of range conquest. He had tried it out in Ruby Valley and on the Bidwell Plains and it had worked smoothly and perfectly in both places. It had seemed foolproof, so he had tried it again, here in the shadow of the Sentinels. And here it had blown up in his face.

Grat Mallory had warned him of this possibility. Things, so Mallory had claimed, were different than in Ruby Valley or on the Bidwell Plains. Here were a different breed of men, with more to fight for. But he hadn't listened to Mallory, or taken heed. Instead, he'd scoffed and pushed his plan ahead, and now it lay in ruins about him.

Pardee Dane had only to turn his head and look out the window to see, over across the compound in the shadow of a shed overhang, a row of still figures laid out. Three of the figures were Grat Mallory, Chess Breshear, and Ace Scarlett, men who had made his great scheme work in Ruby Valley and on the Bidwell Plains. But they were dead now, and the gray shadow of this realization was a cold shroud that seemed to clog Pardee Dane's mind. He forced himself to look at Fraser, Wilcoxon, and Shurtleff, and the stark hostility he met there seemed to press him into a corner. Fraser spoke.

"You would have it, Dane. Bunch Grass Basin wasn't

enough. You and your damned grass greed! You were warned, but you didn't think we meant it. You thought you had us by the short hair, that you were too big for us to handle. Well, now you know that this isn't Ruby Valley and it isn't the Bidwell Plains. We're ready to go further than we have to prove it to you if we have to. Well?"

Pardee Dane fought for time by getting out a perfecto, gnawing the tip off it rather messily, and lighting it with a third match after breaking the other two. His meticulous fastidiousness had deserted him, even, and he knew a gray and bitter anger at himself for letting these men upset him so and for not being able to hide this fact from their boring glances. His words came jerkily, a little thick.

"I had as much right to put cattle into the Sentinels as any man alive. You had no legal right to attack my crew, stampede my herd. I'm no child, to be bulldozed or bluffed. I know my rights."

"Take another look, Dane," growled Dab Shurtleff with his usual heavy bluntness. "Take another look out that window and see what you see. Dead men. You killed them, Dane, just as surely as if you'd pulled the trigger. God damn men like you! You lay the plans and you give the orders, but you stay behind and play it safe with your mangy hide and let better men pay the penalty. So now I tell you this. I never beat around the bush. Fundamentals have always been good enough for me. You stir up another ruckus across this range and I don't fool around with just your hired hands. I come straight at you and I come with a gun in my hand. Remember that!"

Outside, hoofs pounded up, and it was Sheriff Bill Hammer who stepped from a sweating bronc and stood for a moment, cold of eye and face, looking at the row of still figures under the shed overhang. Then he turned on Soddy Joens, who was lounging near by, and shot a couple of harsh questions. After which Hammer came swiftly to the office door, pushed it open, and stepped in.

Immediately Pardee Dane straightened, drawing courage from sight of the sheriff and his star of authority. He tossed his perfecto aside, got out another and lighted it with his old flair. A glint came into his eyes, and he said smoothly, "I'm glad you are here, Sheriff. With your own eyes you see the savage results of an utterly unprovoked attack on my men and—"

"Shut up!" Bill Hammer's words were like the cut of a whip. His glance bored at Cleve Fraser. "Tell me about it."

Fraser did so, tersely direct. Pardee Dane added his say quickly. "You see, Sheriff, he admits it. My men did not attack. It was these men who did that, along with their crews. And I demand redress by law. I shall prosecute to the full." Dane would have said more, but Bill Hammer's coldly bitter stare held and silenced him. And when Dane went still, Hammer spoke, harshly emphatic.

"Let's get one thing clear, Dane. I don't like men like you. I don't like men who, because they happen to have heavy money and influence in certain quarters behind them, set out to stomp on the necks of other men, to grind them down and break them, and then grab off range these men have worked and sweat blood to own and develop. No, I don't like men like that.

"Nor do I like men who hire other men to do the fighting and dying for them, while they sit back to lap up the gravy. Those are my personal sentiments, and I wanted to make them clear so you'll understand once and for all just where you and I stand. Now, here is an official word. The law doesn't look kindly on the man who hires gun fighters and pays them cold cash in advance to gang another man and smoke him down. The law calls that accessory to attempted murder!"

A startled flicker showed far back in Pardee Dane's eyes. He used a moment to touch a freshening match to his perfecto. Then he said, "I must say again that my men did not attack at Tamarack Springs. They were set upon by Fraser and these others."

"I'm not referring to that at all, Dane," said Hammer curtly. "I'm talking of something else. I'm talking about your hiring the Lockyear brothers, Trace and Nolly, to gang Cleve Fraser and shoot him down. They tried just that one day in town, but as it happened it didn't work out as planned. I was there and saw it all. I know what I'm talking about."

The tip of Dane's perfecto glowed with a sudden brightness. "I've been lied about before."

"Maybe, but not this time," rapped Bill Hammer. "You see, I just came from having a long, heart-to-heart talk with the Lockyear brothers. While clearing up that stage-robbery affair I saw several things across this range that needed ironing out. The past, present, and future of the Lockyear brothers' activities was one of these."

Hammer paused to roll a cigarette. He drove a thin line of smoke from his lips and went on.

"You see, Dane, you never can tell just how a man's mind may work. In this case it was Trace Lockyear's thinking that surprised. That day in town Cleve Fraser could have killed Nolly Lockyear and been fully justified. But he didn't. Cleve just shot a leg out from under Nolly and let it go at that. This made a deep impression on Trace Lockyear. He's been thinking about it ever since, and it was a gesture of generosity that Trace just couldn't get over. So he asked me to tell Cleve Fraser that he'd never have any trouble with the Lockyears again, and he admitted flatly that the reason he and Nolly tried to get Cleve that day was because, through Grat Mallory, you had hired them to do it and paid hard cash in advance."

Pardee Dane still hung on to a shred of his self-possession. "The word of an acknowledged cattle thief and general all-around, no-account individual against mine, Sheriff?"

Bill Hammer's laugh was a short mirthless bark. "And is your word pure gold, Dane? Never mind answering that. Trace Lockyear is willing to swear to his statement in court. Said he felt he owed that much to Fraser after Fraser's generous move with Nolly. And the court will always consider seriously the sworn word of any man. So if Cleve Fraser will swear out the warrant, I'm going to slap an arrest on you, Dane. I'm going to put the cuffs on you and drag you out to the lockup at Breed's junction the same as I would any other cheap crook. You may have influence in some quarters, but this range belongs to the men who built it, and in these parts they call the turns."

Pardee Dane here lost that last shred of self-possession and the old sense of trapped desperation deepened. Where was his strength now, where his security? Abruptly he realized how much he'd depended upon Grat Mallory in the past. It was Mallory who had handled the rough edges of the range conquests for him, while he sat back in security. It was Mallory who had done the dirty work, ramrodded the crews, got down in the dust and dirt and sweat and blood and made things move. Why, he had been leaning on Grat Mallory far more than he dreamed, and now Grat wasn't here to lean on any more. Grat Mallory was dead. . . .

Fine sweat beaded Pardee Dane's dry, precise features. He was thinking of the ignominy of being taken to jail in handcuffs. Even if he beat the charge the stigma would still be there. But maybe he wouldn't beat the charge, maybe one of these cow-country juries would send him over the road! Pardee Dane shuddered at the possibility.

Anything like that could be utterly ruinous to him. Not only in the eyes of others, but within himself. For he knew it would kill something in him, wipe out forever the fabric of esteem he'd built up within himself. False that esteem might be to others, and hypocritical, but it was real to Pardee Dane. He had built it up slowly and carefully over the years, and it had been the one citadel of strength that had enabled him to swing other men to his command. It had given him stature beyond his actual right, and he had gloried in it. It was the thing that had made Grat Mallory always refer to him as Mr. Dane, always show him that extra small measure of respect.

Pardee Dane scrubbed a hand across his face. It was hard to realize that Grat Mallory was dead. What would he do with Bunch Grass Basin without Grat to handle the affairs of its widespread acres? Bunch Grass was his, all right. He, Pardee Dane, owned every last foot of it, and as long as he stayed within the limits of it his interests there, whatever they might be, were secure. But, even so, from now on it would be just an island in a sea of never-ending hostility. These men whom he'd set out to wrong and ruin would never forget, and their hatred and enmity would always be stalking at his side.

Abruptly Pardee Dane knew he was whipped. There was a streak of gambler in this man, cold, precise, and merciless when he held the high cards, but one never foolish to call a bet when it was openly obvious that he did not. And he knew now that he didn't hold the high cards in this deal, nor had he ever. His strength was one kind, but the strength of such men as Fraser, Wilcoxon, and Shurtleff was another, and it was greater than his. It was more than just a materialistic strength such as his. Theirs held an element of the spiritual, a part of the earth they walked on and owned and would die fighting to retain. Yes, theirs was the strength of the very land itself.

A good gambler, holding low cards, got out with as little loss as possible. Pardee Dane knew it was time to toss in his hand. His pride, his sense of cocksureness, the presumed infallibility of his planning, all were going to take a beating. This game had gone sour, very sour, and he wanted no more of it. Now, if he could make a trade that would wipe out that threat of arrest . . . !

"What," asked Pardee Dane abruptly, "is Bunch Grass Basin worth to you men?"

For a moment Art Wilcoxon and Dab Shurtleff did not grasp the implications of this startling question. But Cleve Fraser did, and he was quick to give Pardee Dane no chance to overplay a bargaining hand.

"Part of the price will be whether I do or do not swear out that warrant for your arrest, Dane," said Fraser coldly. "Aside from that, considering the improvements you've put in here in this headquarters, plus what you paid for Bunch Grass in the first place, I'd say that fifty thousand dollars would be fair all around."

Pardee Dane met Fraser's narrowed glance and held it for a little time. Here, he thought, was the man whom he'd sensed from the very first would be the one he'd have to whip. And this man had shown that he did not whip easy. Grat Mallory had understood this and had warned him so. Grat had been right and he wrong. Now Grat was dead. As far as it was possible for him to be in any way generous, Pardee Dane was generous enough at this moment to know a touch of real regret about Mallory. For Grat had been faithful.

Dane sighed deeply and nodded. "Very well. Fifty thousand it is. And a clean break on everything else. I'll need a little time to move out the cattle I brought in."

"Agreed," said Fraser. "Fifty thousand and a clean break on all the other angles."

"Fifty thousand!" blurted Dab Shurtleff. "None of us—"

"No, Dab—none of us alone," cut in Fraser. "But

between the four of us, Art and you and Alec Cormack and myself, we can swing it. What we should have done in the beginning we now get around to." He turned to Bill Hammer. "If it's all right with you, Bill, we'll forget that warrant."

The sheriff's face was inscrutable as he nodded. "You're the doctor, Cleve."

Fraser looked at Pardee Dane again. "We'll see you at Burt Statler's law office in Mineral tomorrow morning at ten o'clock and close the deal."

"Ten o'clock it is." Pardee Dane nodded. "I'll be there."

14. *One Man's Future*

THE AFTERNOON WAS RUNNING OUT. SUNLIGHT LAID A strong, flat blaze across Bunch Grass and left a ragged shadow to follow along behind Cleve Fraser as he jogged toward Shield and Cross headquarters. His wounded arm, resting in a sling, felt as well as could be expected. He'd stopped by in town to let Doc Curtain fix it up and Doc had done a good job of it, recommending a couple of days in bed, then adding with profane skepticism, "Damn sound advice which I know you won't take."

Weariness rode with him, but it was a kind of good weariness: the loose-muscled, letdown kind that came after a long period of taut and grinding strain. Looking back, Fraser could see that this strain had begun the day of the government sale of Bunch Grass. On that day had begun a series of incidents and developments which had scattered in fragments an old and fixed and well-remembered pattern of life across this range.

On that day an instinct, a strange, deep-seated awareness had risen in him, telling him that life as he had known it had taken a right-angled turn and the shadow of grim events sure to follow had hovered at his shoulder. And this awareness had not told him wrong.

Violence had come and gone. In many ways things would never be the same, for despite the inevitable cushion of time a man would always remember. People went out of a man's life, others came into it, if only for a little time. A man glimpsed things which made men and women what they were and he wondered, though he never found all the answers.

The abrupt about-face of Pardee Dane was one of the things to wonder at. You wondered if the man was innately a coward, or if it was merely that he was cold-minded enough to recognize a complete checkmate for the present, while seeing a future ahead so full of conflict as to not be worth the price. You wondered over the warning that Pardee Dane's niece had brought and why she had done so.

Fraser thumbed a pocket and brought out a small fold of scented notepaper, which had been enclosed in an envelope that Henry Poe had given him after flagging him down in town. On the envelope had been written simply, "Cleve Fraser."

"She asked me to give it to you at the first chance, Cleve," Henry Poe had said.

Fraser had read the enclosure right after leaving town.

Now he read it again. It ran:

Cleve:

This is good-by. We learn things as we go along, don't we? Mainly that we can't beat life. I am neither as bad as I seemed nor as good as I should be. A woman's heart can lead her to unpredictable things. For you, my dear, the best of everything. And should you ever think of me, do so with kindness.

Sherry

Fraser stared straight ahead for some little distance. Then, wedging the paper between a knee and the swell fork of his saddle, he shredded it carefully to very small pieces with his sound right hand and let the pieces drift to earth. To some things there just simply were no answers. . . .

Except for a gilding fire along the highest reaches of the Sentinels, the sun was gone when Fraser rode up to Shield and Cross. Twilight held the land, and its first cooling breath was a flickering sweetness against a man's face. Well, there were some things that nothing could ever change, the earth and the sky and the fine, far beauty of space. These things were free, and if a man was smart he drew upon them and in their willing bounty found the magic of complete serenity.

Things were quiet at Shield and Cross and a suggestion of the old-time peace was there. But there was grief too. For Concho Payne, a good and faithful Shield and Cross rider, had gone to his death up at Tamarack Springs.

It was Mother Cormack who met Fraser at the door. She was gravely sad, but swiftly concerned. "Your arm, boy, how is it? Sam Tepner told us you'd been wounded."

"It will be a nuisance for a while, but nothing worse," Fraser told her. "And at the end of a day that's been about as rough as any I've ever known I can finally bring some good news, Mother Cormack. Alec will want to hear this."

She followed him into her husband's room. The old cattleman seemed grim and tired as he looked up at Fraser from beneath his shaggy brows.

"Once we talked about what could lie ahead, Cleve— after Pardee Dane moved in on Bunch Grass. Well, it came, and here I had to be old and useless when I'd have given anything to have made that ride with you and the rest of the boys this morning. We paid a price, but we gave them a damn good pushing around, so Sam Tepner says. How's that arm?"

"It'll do," answered Fraser briefly. "News for you, Alec. Pardee Dane has had enough. Bunch Grass is for sale again."

Alec Cormack reared up from his pillow. "What's that? Cleve, do you know what you're saying?"

"I think so. Ease back and listen, Alec." Then Fraser went on to tell all about it. When he finished Alec Cormack exclaimed with a harsh satisfaction.

"Hah! Turned coyote, did he, when the trail began to get real rough? And I'd heard he was a cold proposition, not easy scared."

Fraser shrugged. "A hard man to figure, Alec. Maybe

there's not the starch in him we first figured, or maybe he's just cold-blooded enough gambler to toss in a hand that's gone sour. Or maybe there's some other angle we don't know anything about. None of which really matters a great deal any more. What counts with us is that he's ready to sell and at a price you and I and Art Wilcoxon and Dab Shurtleff can swing between us. Art and Dab are more than willing, of course, and between the four of us we should be able to draw up an ownership and grazing agreement on Bunch Grass that will make everybody happy. If that leg of yours can stand the ride I'll be by tomorrow morning and take you to town in the buckboard."

"Damn right it'll stand the ride. I been telling Sarah there was no good reason for me sticking around this cussed bed any longer. Now I got the best excuse in the world to get out of it. Cleve, I'll be ready!"

Going back to the outer door with Fraser, Mother Cormack noticed his questing glance and manner.

"Les is off riding somewhere, Cleve. I declare if that girl doesn't act like she's possessed. Restless, uneasy, full of fits and starts. I never saw her so. You'd best stay to supper. She'll probably be back shortly."

Fraser shook his head, faintly smiling. "Guess I'm possessed, too, Mother Cormack."

Twilight had become deep dusk by the time Fraser reached the shallows of Stony Creek below the bridge, and he paused to let his horse drink. Halfway through this pleasant moment the dun lifted its head, ears pricked, muzzle dripping. Gravel crunched under other hoofs, and then it was Leslie Cormack's tall sorrel which stood on the far bank, with Les straight and still in the saddle. Fraser rode across.

"Girl," he scolded gently, "you worry folks the way you skitter around. Your mother's fretting right now. Where you been?"

"Saber headquarters. Saw Soddy Joens there and he said you should be along most any time. I waited as late as I dared. I—I wanted to be sure about your arm, Cleve."

As always, this girl's voice was melody in his ears and her presence a deep and fulfilling comfort. For the moment he was content with just these. In the brief silence that fell she studied him. In the saddle he loomed tall and solid against the pale, shy gleam of the first stars.

Les had heard all the story from Soddy Joens, and now in this man before her she saw the rock upon which Pardee Dane's dream of power had smashed. The old tough, gentle Cleve. This man who was solid all the way through, who hewed exactly to the line of his convictions and principles. For so many years she had unconsciously leaned upon his willing strength, not fully realizing the comfort and security it gave.

Well, she knew now. There were so many things she knew now! She went on a trifle hurriedly. "Sam Tepner brought us the first news. I just couldn't stay still after that. I liked Concho Payne. He was a quiet, steady rider. Life costs us all something, Cleve."

"Win or lose, there's a price." Fraser nodded. "Pardee Dane found that out. He's selling out, Les. Tomorrow Bunch Grass Basin comes back to the men who need it."

He went on to explain, and then concluded, "So we end up just where we began, with much missing and nothing added."

She went still again for some little time. Her sorrel stamped a restless hoof, tossed its head, fretting at the snaffle. Les quieted the animal and then said slowly, "Has nothing at all been added, Cleve?"

The way she spoke them, more than the actual words, brought him up straight, staring at her; her tone seemed to throb, like the silent magic voice of warm dusk. It was too dark to read her face, but the shadowy outline of her held all the old and well-remembered grace. There was a quickening inside him.

"Les—what do you mean?"

"Maybe," she said softly, "you think there is a shadow between us, Cleve. There isn't. Things I once thought were true never really were. That day when you faced the Lockyears in town—then I knew the real truth. I knew it—oh, so well."

Fraser swung his horse closer. "But there was Vance, Les. I thought—"

"Yes," she cut in, "there had been Vance. Something that blinded the eyes of both of us—for a time. But something that had never been truly real—not truly. Why, even when I heard of Vance's death the sense of loss was a strangely distant thing. It hurt, of course, but it still left me completely whole. But that day in town, and these past hours, guessing—wondering what was going on up in the mountains—waiting to see you come riding again. Oh, Cleve, don't you understand?" Her voice was shaking, almost tearful.

His sound hand went out, capturing one of hers. How dear she was to him! This fine and honest girl—this lovely playmate, as he had so fondly called her.

"There never has been the need of words to tell you how I've always felt, Les. Always, from the very first!"

Her answer was whisper soft. "I want to hear the words, Cleve."

The stars had brightened to a scattered glinting and down from among them a nighthawk, early awing, poured its cool, pure call. . . .

Center Point Publishing
600 Brooks Road • PO Box 1
Thorndike ME 04986-0001 USA

(207) 568-3717

US & Canada:
1 800 929-9108